W9-CCD-466

DIANNE HAWORTH

Kaimanawa Princess

HarperCollins*Publishers*

National Library of New Zealand Cataloguing-in-Publication Data

Haworth, Dianne.
Kaimanawa Princess / Dianne Haworth
ISBN 978-186950-7046
1. Purcell, Rochelle—Juvenile fiction. [1. Purcell, Rochelle—
Fiction. 2. Wild horses—Fiction. 3. Horses—Fiction.
4. Wildlife conservation—Fiction.] I. Title.
NZ823.3—dc 22

This is a work of fiction. The characters, incidents and dialogues are products of
the author's imagination and are not to be construed as real.

First published 2008
HarperCollinsPublishers *(New Zealand) Limited*
P.O. Box 1, Auckland

Copyright © Dianne Haworth 2008

Dianne Haworth asserts the moral right to be identified
as the author of this work.

All rights reserved. No part of this publication may be reproduced,
stored in a retrieval system or transmitted in any form or by any means,
electronic, mechanical, photocopying, recording or otherwise,
without the prior written permission of the publishers.

ISBN 978 1 86950 704 6

Cover design by Christa Moffitt and Alicia Freile
Cover images: girl and horse by Brooke Fasani/Getty Images;
horse drinking by Pat Powers and Cherryl Schafer/Getty Images
Typesetting by Janine Brougham

Printed by Griffin Press, Australia

50gsm Bulky News used by HarperCollins*Publishers* is a natural, recyclable
product made from wood grown in sustainable plantation forests.
The manufacturing processes conform to the environmental regulations
in the country of origin, New Zealand.

Kaimanawa Princess
is dedicated to the wild horses of
the Kaimanawa Ranges — the wind eaters.

Contents

Acknowledgements *9*

Part One

Chapter 1   **'I want that one!'** *13*

Chapter 2   **'Please phone me back'** *27*

Chapter 3   **'Can you keep a secret?'** *41*

Chapter 4   **'It'll bring good luck'** *57*

Chapter 5   **'We'll show them!'** *73*

Chapter 6   **A theft** *90*

Part Two

Chapter 7   **Plants or horses?** *107*

Chapter 8   **The battle rages** *125*

Chapter 9   **TV star** *140*

Chapter 10 **Showdown on
             the Desert Road** *156*

Acknowledgements

Kaimanawa Princess has been inspired by thirteen-year-old Rochelle Purcell and her pony, Kaimanawa Princess, who captured the heart of the nation in August 1996, for their part in the campaign to save the wild horses of the Kaimanawas when they appeared on television and then participated in the massive protest on the Desert Road.

While this is not Rochelle's own story, I would like to thank her for her help and support in the writing of this book and for sharing with me her experiences of her magnificent little pony. Many of the characters in *Kaimanawa Princess* are fictional, while others in the public eye have been identified in describing the events that took place at that time.

There are many people I wish to thank for sharing their time and energy in bringing the heart-warming story of the Kaimanawa wild horses to light. In particular I would like to acknowledge Roger and Sue Ginsberg, Bob Kerridge, Marilyn and Elder Jenks of the Kaimanawa Wild Horse Welfare Trust, The Franz Weber Foundation, the Leighton family, Roger Dutton, Lucinda Russell, Sid Dickinson, Lisa Bellingham, WHOA and the ever-supportive encouragement of my publishers HarperCollins and Lorain Day.

Dianne Haworth
Auckland, 2008

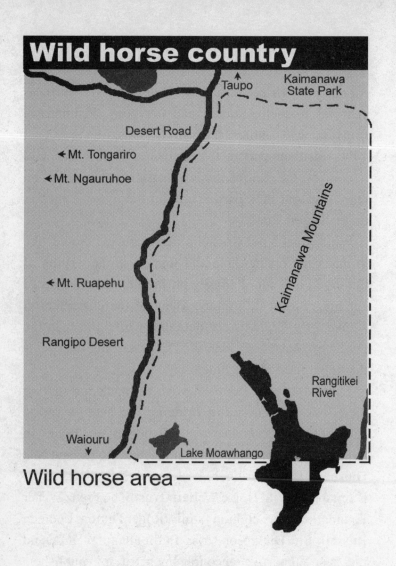

Wild horse country

Taupo

Kaimanawa State Park

Desert Road

◄ Mt. Tongariro

◄ Mt. Ngauruhoe

◄ Mt. Ruapehu

Kaimanawa Mountains

Rangipo Desert

Rangitikei River

Waiouru

Lake Moawhango

Wild horse area – – – –

Part One

Chapter 1

'I want that one!'

It's a brilliantly clear and icy morning with snow capping the majestic Kaimanawa and Central Plateau mountain ranges as a black foal with a small white blaze on her nose and four tiny white socks enters into the world, landing with a soft thud on the springy golden-brown tussock grass.

Close by the newborn and her mother, who is protectively licking her baby clean, three mares and two foals hover, whinnying softly, while at a distance their stallion keeps a watchful eye — if any danger presents itself he will step forward and place himself between the predator and his family.

The stallion has spent time this day, as he does every day, with each individual in his band — focusing his energies in particular on the two male foals who are inseparable, and happy to pass their time in repeated sessions of boisterous neck wrestling. Is he teaching them how to — one day — become stallions themselves and so to become responsible for caring for their own bands of mares and foals in the sanctuary of their mountain kingdom?

The band spends up to twenty hours each day grazing together and socialising, some resting, while others keep watch to warn of any danger. Each mare has her own special friend who she likes to spend more time with than the others, taking it in turns to mind each other's foals so that all can enjoy some rest time free of the responsibilities of motherhood and graze for the succulent herbs or grasses.

As soon as the baby learns to suckle from her mother and can walk without wobbling on her long, gangly legs, this band of horses will be off, galloping freely across the wild and craggy inhospitable country that they — and 130 previous generations of the tough Kaimanawa ponies descended from the wild ponies of Exmoor and Wales introduced to New Zealand in 1876 — call home.

Through a fog of steam rising from the terrified wild horses huddled together in the hastily constructed saleyards, Becky saw her standing alone, a beautiful small black Kaimanawa pony with four white socks and a distinctive white blaze that ran the length of her nose.

'I want that one!' Becky demanded, pointing across the fenced stock paddock to where she stood.

'What's the rush?' her dad asked. 'There are heaps to choose from, Becks, we've come a long way to pick a pony for you, and there might be others that are much more suitable . . .'

'I want *that* pony — I don't want to look at anyone else, she's gorgeous!' Becky was digging her toes in, determined to get her own way.

Her mother sighed. This could bring on another row between two of the strong-minded characters she lived with. Better to hop in now and defuse the situation.

'Look, you two.' Toni Mitchell pointed towards a large man in jeans and a checked shirt who was wandering in their direction. 'Here's a guy who seems to know what's going on — I'll ask him if he can tell us anything about that pony's history.'

As a matter of fact, he could. Paul Grant nodded in answer to her question. 'Funny you should single that pony out, folks, because I work as a helicopter pilot and she was in one of the bands I rounded up from the Argo Valley down by the Army camp. I brought them a hell of a long way to get here . . . and I won't forget this little group because . . .' He paused, squinting his eyes in the direction of the horses. 'Yep! There she is — that determined old girl who may well be your pony's mother. She's obviously past her prime and all the way she struggled to keep up with the rest of her band. I tried to separate her from them, by closing in on her with the copter's blades whirring above as close as I could get, to frighten her off.'

'Why did you want to do that?' Becky was indignant. 'Horses in their own groups always want to stick together!'

'Ah yes, but—' Should he tell the kid the ugly truth or keep quiet? Aw, what the heck. 'Well, I was trying to protect her because I like horses, and she was such a plucky mare. I knew what her fate would be when she came down here to the saleyards . . .'

'What's that?' Becky followed his gaze. 'Tell me!'

'Well, as you probably know, this is the first ever Kaimanawa horse muster, ordered by the powers-that-be and the conservationists. The young horses like your pony will find homes if they're lucky, but the older ones like her and the stallions will be sent off to the meat works, because they won't fetch anything from buyers. All that journey over the mountains and loyal effort from her for a pretty harsh fate . . .'

'No! We'll take her too!' Becky's eyes filled with tears. 'My pony will need her own Kaimanawa friend in her paddock and her mother will be the best one to make her feel better about losing her freedom.'

'Steady on, Becky!' Her father's voice rose in alarm. 'Look, I'm a dairy farmer, not a charity. We agreed to pay $100 for your pony, but buying a useless old mare as well is just plain stupid. The answer is no.'

'How much would the mother go for?' Becky turned her back on her father and addressed Paul. 'I'll pay for her myself with my savings.'

16

This was getting embarrassing, Paul thought, looking from the girl's mutinous face to her parents' dismay. 'Um, well, I suppose fifty dollars would buy her, but then there's the upkeep . . .'

'*Pleeaaase*, please, please, pretty please Mum and Dad.' Becky's brown ponytail swung from side to side as she faced first one parent and then the other. 'After school, I'll work on the farm for you every week to pay for her hay and barley. Just let me have them both — it can be my birthday present — and I'll groom and care for them so well, you won't believe it.'

'Your birthday isn't for another four months,' Toni laughed. 'Well, we've brought our double horse float, so that must have been an omen . . . and I quite like the idea of rescuing her mum too. It brought a lump to my throat hearing about her following her daughter across that wild country! It's OK by me — what do you say, Bruce?'

He was outnumbered, may as well give in gracefully. 'OK, OK. You win, we'll take the old girl too, but mind, Becky, I'm going to hold you to that promise. Starting tomorrow you hose down the milking shed every afternoon, OK?'

'OK, Dad,' Becky beamed.

Paul Grant smiled. These were the kind of people he liked. It had been upsetting enough for a guy like him who had grown up with horses to have to round them up to face an uncertain fate, but days like this made it all worthwhile. These two animals would number among the lucky ones.

'I'll take you across to Jack who's selling the horses.' Paul swung off the fence he was leaning on as they talked. 'You can settle up with him, then if you back your float up to that gate, I'll get a couple of the guys to rope your two up and bring them over for loading onto your truck.

'I know you're horse people, but, I've got to warn you,' he added, 'these Kaimanawas aren't used to humans. They're wild and the only life they know is roaming the ranges, often through some pretty harsh weather. And when they come from the Argo Valley, like your two, they react badly to gunshots or loud sounds because their territory runs by the army's firing range.

'The Kaimanawas are natural survivors who have adapted brilliantly to their environment. They're pretty independent and clever, so you'll have an interesting time breaking them in.'

Paul had a suggestion to make if the mare and her daughter failed to settle in their new environment. 'There's a strange sort of bloke who's lived and worked with the Kaimanawa horses for years on an old sheep station in the northern part of the territory. He's supposed to be something of a horse-whisperer and he can break Kaimanawas in quickly because he's so used to their ways . . . his name is Bill Worth.

'Don't be put off by his weird looks — he's a real cracker. Here's my phone number.' He scribbled down some numbers on a dirty scrap of paper and handed it to Becky. 'Give me a call if you need him. You'll never find Bill under your own steam, but I know people who'll

18

track him down for you and — if he chooses to help you — he'll come up to your place and sort it. You don't need to worry about giving Bill a bed or lodgings or even money for the work he'll do. He's a law unto himself and lives in a funny old grey bus with his best mate, a dog called Bro . . .'

Becky smiled to herself. It was unlikely she'd need Bill's help. After all, she was eleven now and had been riding since she was two. She'd never failed with a horse yet and she wasn't about to start.

Her new pony was going to be her best friend . . . carrots, chunks of apple, understanding and lots of love would calm her down and then with some help from their neighbour, Tom Jackson, she'd secretly prepare her to meet the world at the pony club.

Looking at her daughter's happy face, Toni smiled. 'Well, honey, you heard the warning but — knowing you — that'll just make you more determined to succeed. Any ideas on a name yet?'

Becky gazed across at the pony. 'Yes. I'm going to call her Kaimanawa Princess, because she'll be the princess of our Ribbon Days and the Pony Club show.'

'Well, if she's going to be a princess we should call her mother Queenie.' Toni grinned. 'Good choice, Becky . . .'

'Right!' Bruce Mitchell started moving towards the saleyard. 'Enough chat. I'm going to pay the man over there and then we'll load your precious Kaimanawa Princess and old Queenie onto the float. And then we're off — I've seen enough of this unhappy carry-on for one day. I want to get home so we can settle the two of them in the back paddock before dark.'

They have been rounded up, trapped without food, crammed together and frightened. They have seen their stallion and other horses disappearing and been put in front of people they've never seen before — the men who are herding them are their first ever human contact. Both the pony and the mare, with their teeth gnashing, are struggling wildly as unfamiliar ropes are tightened around their necks.

'Grrrup,' snarls one of the handlers, aiming a swing at Queenie with a long prodding stick, 'you're lucky to be alive! If I had my way you and your lot would be off to the meat works.'

Stumbling, snorting and struggling against the shoves and prods coming their way from both front and behind, the mare and her pony are dragged up the small ramp and into the blackness of the horse float.

Happy that her two new horses were safely on board, Becky climbed into the back seat as Bruce Mitchell carefully manoeuvred his way clear of the gates, across a muddy paddock and out onto the main road north. Soon she was asleep, sprawled across the back seat of the station wagon, oblivious to the thumpings and bangings in the float behind them.

The restlessness of the horses was making the float unstable and Bruce was worried. The sooner this journey was over, the better. 'I don't know if this was such a good idea,' he muttered to his wife. 'These horses could be a real handful from what that guy Paul was saying.'

'Look, Bruce.' Toni had been through this argument a number of times. 'You know with the mortgage on our farm we can't afford to pay thousands of dollars to replace old Binky. He might have another few months at the pony club, but he's starting to trip at events and at twenty he's earned an honourable retirement.

'Becky's a great little rider and she's not a greedy kid. There's only one thing she has ever wanted and that's a horse of her own she can train up from scratch.

'The Kaimanawas come cheap because they've never been rounded up and sold before, so no one knows what they're like . . . and, yes, they're small and wild with shaggy coats, but we'll get there and — don't forget, Bruce — Tom's offered to help Becky break her pony in and with jumps work in the paddock. He's retired and has lots of time on his hands and you haven't!'

Bruce stared at the road ahead and let his mind wander. For eight years they'd worked hard as sharemilkers on the dairy farm, and just months earlier they'd been given the chance to buy it outright. It had come at a huge expense, but thanks to their bank manager the loan had just been approved. There wasn't much left over for any luxuries, and as far as he was concerned, these two ponies fell into the luxury bracket.

He agreed that there were some pluses. Owning a pony would keep Becky out of trouble and if she truly wanted to become a top rider there was no better way to start than with a pony she would be able to train up and keep for years.

Binky, their old gelding, would have some company in his old age, and probably the biggest bonus of all was the fact that the previous owners of their farm had a horse-mad son. A decade before they'd set up a large paddock with safety post-and-rail fences and gate, and an open shed for the ponies to shelter from the driving rain during the winter months and the sun in summer. There was a large water trough alongside the shed and enough space for end-to-end jumps practice . . . more money saved.

Within the darkness of the float, Kaimanawa Princess was almost driving herself to exhaustion. Terrified of the unfamiliar surroundings she struggled to escape from the cramped space that had her trapped. By now she was hungry and parched with thirst — craving for great long gulps of clear, fresh water from the icy mountain streams of her wild home.

Where was she being taken? She pushed forward into the darkness, neighing with fear. In the box next to her daughter, Queenie was also whinnying and deeply frightened. She longed for their stallion to put some order back into their lives, but he had been separated from them. At the saleyards she'd tried to bite the handlers to show them what she thought of being imprisoned, but they were too crafty for her, though she had succeeded in ripping a large hole in one man's jersey.

Finally her daughter's fear and her own longing for comfort prompted the mare's next move. Inclining her head towards the next box, Queenie gently nudged Kaimanawa Princess. It wasn't much of a gesture, but it seemed to calm them both. Whatever strange fate the pair were destined for, at least they were together.

At intermediate school on Monday morning, Becky's best friend, Rachel Montgomery, rushed up to her. 'Did you get the pony you wanted?'

'Shhhh — it's a secret!' Becky cautioned. 'I'm not telling anyone except you that I've got a new pony. She's so cute and I love her, though she's still very frightened and won't let me near her. I don't want those snotty kids at pony club knowing we've bought a cheap Kaimanawa horse. They'd all laugh at us, especially that bossy Danielle.

'I'm going to train her up and then I'll take her to the pony club and big sucks to them when she beats their flash ponies!'

She wanted Rachel to see her pony as soon as possible

though, she added hastily, 'Can you come over after school on your bike and we'll go down to the back paddock to see her? *And* I've bought her mother, too!'

Then Becky remembered. 'Oh, blow, I promised Dad I'd hose out the milking shed every day after school in return for being allowed to keep her mother — Mum's called the old mare Queenie, because I've called my pony Kaimanawa Princess. So now we've got a Queen and a Princess!'

'Can't anyway.' Rachel turned away. 'Things aren't too good at home at the moment, so I've got to be there for the younger kids when they get home from primary school. Mum is still threatening to walk out. She says she's going for better work than she's got here, but I reckon the real reason is that she's got a boyfriend . . . I heard her on the phone. And Dad, well, Dad's got grumpy and he just keeps drinking beer . . .'

'Oh no.' What else could she say? 'OK, not to worry.' Becky gave Rachel a quick hug as the bell rang and they returned to their classes. Becky felt so sorry for her friend, and so grateful that this was something she didn't have to face at home. As she looked over at Rachel's sad expression, she determined to try and think of some way to help her friend.

Before they had driven down to the Central Plateau to find her Kaimanawa pony, Becky's neighbour Tom Jackson — an experienced horseman — had promised he would break in the new pony. But first, he told her, they had to leave the pony in peace to settle into unfamiliar surroundings in a paddock.

The temptation to go over to Queenie and Princess was almost too much for Becky to stand. That afternoon, wearing her old jeans and a T-shirt to hose out the milking shed, she decided to detour on her way to the shed so she could see her two ponies. There they were, standing together under the big tree in the far corner of their paddock . . .

As she stared at them, Becky wondered what it would be like to spend your whole life climbing or cantering in the mountains, roaming together, grazing wherever you felt like, with no rules, no nothing . . . and then find your life confined to just one flat Bay of Plenty paddock without any hills for miles around and be expected to know how to behave in a human's world. 'I think I would find that pretty scary,' she admitted to herself.

She remembered what she'd read the week before in her horse manual about caring for ponies and understanding them. She couldn't remember exactly what it said but it talked about how humans put horses in situations which challenge their instincts. The book went on to say how important it was for your horse to know that you understand its needs. The part she had especially liked said there was a line of communication between a horse and its rider and that even when they're scared a horse will always respect your personal space and only go as far or as fast as you ask. She also remembered a bit that talked about the fact that while a horse will always be responsible for placing its own feet, it looks to its rider for guidance when it feels uncomfortable. Becky sighed, wondering how long it would take for her to have that sort of communication with Kaimanawa Princess. She hoped it would be soon . . .

Meanwhile she'd better get on with her work. Becky waved parting kisses over towards the pair, who were now gazing in her direction. 'I'm going to make you two a promise that comes straight from my heart,' she whispered. 'You're going to have the best life I can make for you and I will try my best to understand your every need. But I need you to help me, too! Otherwise my dad will get mad with the three of us and make me sell you both . . . and I couldn't stand for that to happen.'

Chapter 2

'Please phone me back'

Tom Jackson stood at one corner of the paddock scratching his head. The two ponies just wouldn't let themselves be caught, rearing up, baring their teeth and showing great dodging skills — even the little one, just a little over fourteen hands high, was proving a real handful. She was clearly terrified, and fear was turning her nasty, opening her mouth and coming straight for him, forcing him to dodge out of her way.

Watched by Becky on the other side of the fence, Tom tried to approach Queenie and Princess with two halters. They needed to be fitted to get the ropes attached before he could start lunging them in circles — first at a walk, then at a trot and finally at a canter, in their first steps towards being trained.

The problem was, he admitted to himself, this pair was completely unused to any contact with humans and both were obviously fearful. He guessed the pony was about two years old and the mare could be anything . . . Earlier that day Becky had said both had gone berserk when a truck had back-fired on the road past the Mitchells' farm. Clearly they were frightened by explosions and loud noises.

Tom knew there were two opinions about the best way to break in a horse, and he reckoned he sat square in the middle between the two. Some people believed you had to break the will of the horse by violent methods to let them know who was boss — and the opposite camp argued that to get trust and cooperation from horses, you needed to show kindness and patience.

One thing Tom knew for sure — a horse must learn that the cost of an attempted bite or kick at a human is a prompt and measured payback. That generally meant a cuff on the muzzle for a bite and a swat with a switch for a kick. He walked steadily towards Queenie, holding the halter and rope in one hand, a treat in the other and making soothing sounds in her direction as he approached.

The mare looked warily at the man and his out-stretched hand holding a titbit of bread and almost allowed herself to be lured into acceptance. Almost, but not quite. At just two body lengths away from him, she was off, snorting, tossing her head and galloping to the other end of the paddock.

'I'm awfully sorry Mr Jackson,' Becky apologised an hour later as Tom prepared to call it a day. 'They're lovely ponies really, I think it might just take some time . . .'

'Well, Becky, I think you're right about that!' he grinned. 'And, to be honest, I don't know if I'm really the man for you. The horses my kids had were already half broken in by the time we got them, so I never had to start from scratch.

'By the way,' he added, 'our kids have grown up, but we've still got a lot of their tack, their rugs and a couple of good saddles in the shed. I know you've got lots of gear you use for Binky, but come on over and see us for afternoon tea one weekend soon. I've already polished the saddles up in case you want them, and one will be just the right size for you to use with young Princess!'

As he jumped into his ute Tom noticed Becky's head had gone down in dismay at the failure of yet another session. 'There's no doubt about it, you've got a couple of good ones here. Once they're broken in and they've been trained they'll be top little ponies. They're both very bright and when they're ready to learn you'll be away. Just look at the way Princess careers around the paddock, leaping just for the fun of it! She looks like a real champ in the making to me.'

Becky was grateful for his kind comments, but smart enough to realise that this was his nice way of politely bowing out of Princess and Queenie's training . . . what on earth was she going to do now? And then she remembered.

29

Becky ran inside and into her bedroom, where she rummaged through the pockets of the jeans and jacket she'd worn when they drove south to buy Kaimanawa Princess. There! A grubby piece of paper was uncrumpled and on it she read a couple of phone numbers. She'd try Paul Grant on his mobile first.

'Is that Paul?' she asked as a gruff voice responded. 'I don't know if you remember me from when we bought my pony, Kaimanawa Princess, and the old mare we've called Queenie down at the saleyards? My name's Becky Mitchell and you told me you know a really good horse-whisperer who can break in Kaimanawa horses . . . Could you ask him if he'll come up here and help me? I really need him.'

Her older brother Tim was walking down the hall and although they were great mates, she wasn't in the mood to be teased about her ponies. Becky hurriedly finished her call. 'Here's my phone number. Please phone me back and help me. *Soon*!'

By six thirty the following Saturday morning Becky was up and dressed and hard at work preparing Binky, or Mr Binks to use his show name, for her pony club's final Ribbon Day of the season.

Megan, her best friend at the pony club, was the proud owner of Pixie, a fourteen-year-old black-and-white Pinto pony who was one of the stars at local events, and both girls knew each would be trying hard to end the season on a high note.

Megan and Becky had joined the pony club together when they were seven and both had immediately been noticed as riders with real potential by their first instructor, Mrs Kingi. Both girls easily passed their first test — the New Zealand D Grade certificate — and then a couple of years later the harder C Grade qualification, under their new instructor, Mrs Williams, who had been a national champion when she was a teenager.

But today, while Megan would be hoping to add to her bedroom wall's impressive collection of rosettes, certificates and ribbons, Becky concentrated on turning out and presenting her handsome chestnut Binky. At 14.4 hands high, Binky — who had two short white socks on his front legs and a matching white star where the forelock of his mane met his nose — had been a great and loyal friend to her over the past few years.

And, while her wall wasn't covered with horse-and-rider glory like Megan's, the gelding had still picked up his fair share of placed or highly commended ribbons, plus the occasional and much treasured winner's red rosette for eventing and a blue ribbon second placing for Best Turned Out at the end of last season.

Affectionately, Becky stroked her pony's neck and started in on the serious business of grooming. She washed him, plaited his mane and tail, picked out his feet to remove any lumps of grass that had lodged there and then, while he stood patiently, oiled his feet inside and out and put talcum powder on his two white socks. 'Today's special, Binky,' she told him. 'Lower your head because I have to concentrate to get the talcum powder in exactly the right spot at the top of your nose. There — beautiful white again. You're going to look extra smart. Watch out, because you'll have all the girls chasing you!'

For an extra-professional look she made a pattern of diamonds on Binky's hind quarters with a water-brush, sponged his eyes and nostrils, wiped some baby oil around his muzzle and today — for his last public appearance at the club — she had even borrowed her mother's mascara to make those wonderful brown eyes of his look even better with a splendid fringe of long black lashes.

She felt sort of guilty about not sharing her secret news about the Kaimanawa ponies with Megan, who was a pupil at the local convent school and only saw Becky at the pony club or at weekends, but she knew Megan just couldn't keep things to herself.

However hard her friend tried to keep it quiet, by the end of that day the word would be out and everyone at the pony club would know about her Kaimanawa ponies, including Mrs Williams, her instructor. Becky liked Mrs Williams, and knew she would be annoyed to think Becky had kept her news about the ponies to herself.

Why was she being so secretive? It wasn't as though she felt anything but happy and proud about her new ponies . . . well, if she was really honest, the truth was that more than anything else on earth Becky wanted Kaimanawa Princess and Queenie to prove themselves to her before she introduced them to the scrutiny of her friends and her opponents at the pony club.

There! Binky looked a treat with his ears pricked, bright eyes and a coat so shiny you could almost see your reflection in it. 'You look absolutely gorgeous Mr Binks,' she murmured as she finished her handiwork.

With a final pat and kiss on the neck Becky ran across the paddocks to the house for breakfast and a quick shower. Then it was on with her jodhpurs, riding boots, shirt, tie, pony club vest and a tie for her hair before grabbing her saddle, bridle and helmet to wait outside at the gate with Binky for Megan's family to collect them.

Becky's parents were too busy on the farm to be there for the morning flat classes, but they had promised they would be there in time for lunch and the afternoon jumping competitions.

It was a blazing hot morning as Becky joined Megan in the back seat of the ute, with Pixie and Binky safely installed in the horse float behind, their legs bandaged so that they couldn't hurt themselves on the journey. 'Well girls, do you feel lucky today?' Megan's father asked.

'Of course we do!' they laughed. 'Between Pixie and Binky we're going to clean up!'

They arrived at the A & P Showgrounds, where the pony club always held its final competition day and checked in at the show secretary's tent to collect their numbers and see who was competing in each event.

'Becky, let's go over to Jo and Suzy and get them to join us for the Flag Relay race!' Megan was bursting with excitement, competitions were just the best days in her mind — it was so boring when the season was over. 'I reckon we could win. That's one set of ribbons we'll be able to take home! I'm going to do the showjumping event with Pixie — do you want to walk around the course with me?' Becky smiled. Of course she did!

It was probably too risky for Binky, who had tripped and baulked at two of the jumps the last time they entered the showjumping, so today she would keep her four-legged friend's feet firmly on the ground.

Instead they would concentrate on the first event, the Best Turned Out competition, then later on go in the Pole Bending race and Tip and Out. Then there was a really fun event, the Potato Race, and finally a flat-out effort riding at No. 2 in their team's Flag Relay.

But come next season, watch out! She and Kaimanawa Princess would be a real force to be reckoned with, both on the jumps and the flat, she grinned to herself.

Megan and Becky were halfway around their walk of the showjumping course when they saw Danielle approaching with a smirk on her face. As usual, she was immaculately dressed and looked especially good in a new and obviously expensive riding jacket that fitted so brilliantly it had to have been made just for her. Her parents thought nothing of throwing heaps of money in Danielle's direction to make sure their precious child won everything she entered.

34

'Hi there you two.' She tossed a casual glance in their direction. 'Walking the course, huh? You're not entering Binky in the showjumping round are you Becky, not after his last failure? I heard from the secretary that this is his last event,' she added with a small smile. 'Shame . . . and I hear you don't have a new pony to take his place. Perhaps Megan will share Pixie with you.'

Just shut up, Danielle, thought Becky, throwing a furious glance at her, but it was Megan who answered angrily. 'Don't be so mean, Danielle. It's hard enough for Becky that her pony is coming to the end of his career without you sticking your big snout into her business. And yes, Miss Nosey Parker, if you really want to know about next season, Becks and I are going to share Pixie until she finds another pony!'

Sharing Pixie had never been mentioned, but Becky was so grateful for her friend's generous words she almost broke her silence. Today wasn't the right time but, as soon as she could, Megan would be the first to know about her new pony.

As expected, Danielle shone in the dressage rounds and the club's best young horseman, fourteen-year-old Ross Edwards, was in top form over the jumps. But this also turned out to be a great day for Pixie and Binky.

It had started brilliantly for Becky and Mr Binks in the opening event, the Best Turned Out competition. The field had been whittled down to the judges' call for the finalists to present themselves . . .

'Number 422,' the loudspeaker boomed. 'Finalist for

Best Turned Out trophy.' Danielle smoothed down her jacket as her horse Rajah pawed the ground nervously, then glancing sideways at Becky, she prepared to enter the ring.

It seemed to go on for ever. Becky's mouth was dry with nerves as she waited her turn, while glancing around the fenced area. There were her parents, who had arrived early, standing in the background waving. Realising they might break her concentration, their arms went down as they stood with the crowd of spectators who had gathered around the show ring.

'Number 372.' Becky was jolted out of her daydream. That was their number!

'C'mon, Mr Binks — go out in style and show your class,' she muttered in his ear as they broke into a slow trot for the parade in front of the judges, who walked forward to smooth him over and pat for dust before looking at Becky and checking her tack and presentation . . . Mr Binks did everything expected of him.

She didn't have the beautiful jacket and expensive saddle, but she knew that she looked good in her regular outfit and Binky's saddle and chestnut coat shone like a mirror in the sunlight. Now, their appearance was over and they had to wait for the judges' verdict which, they said — as a change from the club's usual routine — would be announced at a prize-giving ceremony at the end of Ribbon Day.

By the middle of the afternoon Pixie and Megan had picked up a first and a third ribbon. Binky won a green ribbon fourth placing in the Sack Race and then showed his great spirit in the Potato Race by tearing up to the bucket at full speed for Becky to throw the potato in and fly on to the line to record the second-fastest time. Another blue ribbon for her bedroom wall and with the Flag Relay and the judges' announcement of the Best Turned Out still to go.

Jo got them off to a flying start in the relay, leaning over and picking up the flag without pausing, before galloping back to hand over to Becky and Mr Binks. 'Go Binky! Go Becks!' the team screamed.

'*No*!' Binky seemed to lose his footing as they turned. '*Keep going*!' Becky shrieked as the rider and horse on their left closed in on them. Miraculously Binky found another gear, rallied and galloped faster than he had for years towards Suzy at No. 3 and their flag handover.

'Binks, you wonderful brave boy.' Becky's voice choked as she fought back the tears and slid her body off his back. 'I think you've hurt your foot, but we'll get it right very soon. I love you darling brave Binky.'

Suzy had held their lead and now it was down to each top horse and rider to fight for victory in the prestigious team trophy. Megan and Pixie, Ross and Tara, Danielle and Rajah, Jackie and Proud Basil . . .

The noise was deafening as first Ross, then Danielle, closed in on Megan and Pixie. But the sight of Danielle from the corner of her eye was the trigger Megan needed. She wasn't going to let Danielle take the race after beating her and Pixie in the jumping ring.

Digging her heels in hard on Pixie's side, Megan stuck her head down to within inches of her pony's ear. 'C'mon, c'mon, carrots for ever if you win . . . Good girl — we're going to do it!'

Yeehah! Jo, Suzy and Becky clustered around Megan and Pixie — everyone talking and laughing at the same time. The Flag Trophy was theirs to keep until the next season and four red ribbons for Jo, Becky, Suzy and Megan to take home.

There was just one announcement left to make. 'And now for the the winner of Best Turned Out . . .' The judge paused. 'This was a difficult decision as there were several immaculate entries. However, the judges have unanimously decided to award the ribbon and trophy to Rebecca Mitchell and her pony Mr Binks.'

Becky thought her heart would explode with pride. She carefully made her way forward, leading a limping Binky to receive the red ribbon that would be hers for ever. 'Don't get too big for your boots, old boy,' she whispered in his ear. 'It was the mascara that did it.'

'Do you know some guy with a strange voice called Bill Worth?' Tim asked Becky as the Mitchells arrived home in triumph. 'I've just had this really weird call. He asked for you, and says he's on his way up to stay with us to sort out your ponies.'

'What on earth are you talking about, Tim?' Toni demanded, looking at her son. 'And who is Bill Worth, Becky?'

'Wow! Awesome! Don't you remember, Mum?' Becky was all persuasion. 'He's the horse-whisperer man that Paul Grant told us about down at the saleyards when we bought Princess and Queenie. Well, I spoke to Paul and he offered to contact him for us.' That wasn't exactly true, but near enough. 'Bill doesn't charge anything because he loves Kaimanawa horses and he lives in an old converted bus with his dog, Bro . . . Tim, when did he say he's coming?'

'Um, I think he said he was on his way now and will be with us tomorrow afternoon. I gave him road directions to get to us—'

Bruce roared. 'Does nobody tell me anything? Who organised this? You, Becky? You don't know anything about this fellow. He could be a sponger, a thief, we might never get rid of him and he could be useless! Well, he can go as fast as he comes!'

'Dad, please give him a couple of days.' As she clutched her ribbons and trophy, Becky felt her fantastic day was evaporating fast. 'If he's no good, send him packing but I've got a feeling he'll be just great. And he doesn't even want money to help me and the ponies! Please, Dad, give him a chance. Don't ruin today for me please, it's one of the happiest in my life and who knows, he might even be able to sort out Binky's foot without us having to pay for a vet.'

Bruce stared doubtfully at his daughter. The fellow was on his way. Fact. He had a reputation with Kaimanawa horses. Fact. He was self-sufficient and lived in his bus with his dog and wouldn't be a financial drain. Fact. OK. He'd go along with it. Put the guy's bus somewhere out in the paddock near the ponies and give it a couple of days. He'd know whether Worth was straight up or not by the end of that time.

'I never seem to win these battles with you, Becky,' her father shrugged. 'All right, he can come and stay, but I warn you, I'll be watching closely.'

Chapter 3

'Can you keep a secret?'

Becky was walking to the milking shed when a cloud of dust enveloped their farm's clay road and the spluttering roar of an old bus stopped her in her tracks.

He had arrived as promised, late in the afternoon. She was so excited that all other thoughts flew out of her head. Rushing back to the front of the house where the bus had jolted to a halt, she yelled at its driver, 'Hi, I'm Becky, and thank you so much for coming. You're my life saver! Follow me and I'll show you where you can park your bus in the paddock.'

'OK.' The voice was languid. 'Lead the way, girlie.'

Minutes later the two were sizing up each other. He saw a young girl with a long brown ponytail and a sprinkle of freckles splattered across her nose and cheeks. She saw a leathery-brown man with wispy grey shoulder-length hair and piercing green eyes, sporting an Australian grazier's hat with dried sweat bands, a faded check shirt and pale blue jeans that had seen better days — clothes, she was to discover, that never changed.

'Well.' Bill looked beyond her to the Kaimanawas' paddock. 'So there they are. I've been breaking them in since I was fourteen and that was a good while ago. I won't have any problems with this pair,' he said. 'You chose well there, girlie. I like the look of them both . . . but I won't be rushing them.

'They've noticed me and that's enough for now. *Bro*!' he called inside the bus. 'Come on out and meet this girlie, she lives at our new home. What's your name again, dear? You're not worried about dogs, are you?'

No, of course she wasn't Becky replied, as a golden Labrador cross waddled down the bus steps towards them. 'Hi Bro, you might frighten the cows or I'd take you down to meet Dad. Ooh! That reminds me.' She bit her lip. 'I've got to go and hose out the milking shed right now so I'll see you later. Mum says, can you come over for a meal with us tonight and meet the family?'

'Yeah, I reckon I can manage that.' He tipped back his hat and grinned at her. 'I'll just settle myself in here on my deck chair where the ponies can get used to seeing me, have a quiet smoke and join you folks later . . .'

In the old days he would often sneak through to Hihitahi with a couple of blokes — Jim Harkness, who hunted rabbits and deer, and Abe, a Maori shepherd who was brilliant with sheep dogs, to spirit some of the horses away from their home in the Kaimanawas to work and live with them on the old 82,000-acre sheep and dairy station at the northern end of the ranges.

Bill Worth leaned over to reach out for more bread to mop up the gravy on his plate. 'They're stocky sturdy little horses, the Kaimanawas, and we used them as our working horses, because they could handle the harsh climate conditions.

'They came free because we used to pinch them for general farm use, and we used to say they were our hack, pack and pull team.' Bill snorted with laughter. 'They were great. We harnessed them to our sleds for carrying the fence posts round the station and they were perfect for the dairy side of things, dragging milk and cream churns up to the front gates. Mostly though, we used them for mustering sheep . . . and we worked them hard.'

When she could get a word in, Toni asked if he would like a second helping of meat. Like the rest of the family — Bruce, Tim, Becky and young Stephanie — Toni was spellbound at the astonishing stories that came tumbling out of their entertaining guest.

Not hearing her, Bill continued. 'The first two horses I broke in were when I was fourteen years old and they were Kaimanawas. I've handled dozens of them since, and I've never ever failed to get them to respond quickly to my methods. Kaimanawas are heavy-legged with big backsides, square heads and whiskers under the chin and mostly they're bay in colour, brown or chestnut.

'They're also very agile, they can jump like stags. I remember one little fella only just fourteen hands jumping over a deer fence, which is pretty high! They could jump over cattle stops that would defy other horses if they felt like it. They were a self-sufficient lot too, we didn't need to put out feed for them as they grazed on grass.'

Bill told them that the station he worked on was one of the first to take up aerial top dressing, and the owner had an old American car with big running boards that his dog used to ride in. Then there was an eccentric Russian who arrived from nowhere one day and just stayed on for years. He continued, 'I liked my life there but my trouble is I've always had wandering feet — in my time I've broken in horses and even camels in the Australian desert.'

Bill kept them entertained with stories about his camel-breaking days, then just as abruptly as he had appeared on their doorstep, he rose to his feet. 'Past my bedtime and time I turned in for the night, folks. Thanks for the meal, and would you happen to have any good-sized raw bones I can take back to Bro, lady?

'And girlie,' he turned to Becky, 'don't worry about those ponies of yours, I won't be going near them for a few days, but I'll be spending plenty of time watching them and they'll be doing the same back to me. We're just getting used to each other.

'I had a look at that other horse of yours this afternoon after you'd left — he's got a slight sprain but there's an infection set in that's holding up his recovery. If it's OK with you, I'll hop over to the milking shed tomorrow morning and get some cow dung. It's an old Aussie bush remedy and it usually sorts out any infection within a day or two.'

Bill walked to the door and then turned back to Becky. 'You need to treat horses with the same respect you treat humans and that's what I'm showing your Kaimanawas now, by not rushing them. They'll be as smart as the rest of their breed, and will turn out to be everything that you want. You'll see.' And with a cheery wave, he left the room.

'Well!' Bruce was the first to speak, after Toni returned to the table from the kitchen where she'd wrapped some beef bones for Bro in newspaper. 'That was something pretty unusual . . . he's either the biggest con man on earth, or he's everything he says he is — a genius around horses. I must say I liked him . . .'

Did she want to go for a ride on the beach? The school holidays had just begun and Megan was on the phone. 'Is Binky's foot OK?'

'Yes, yes, yes to a ride on the beach!' Like Megan, Becky lived for the holidays when they could ride around together on their horses and race each other along the water's edge along the wonderful golden sandy beach that fronted their farms. 'And hopefully yep to Binky being all right. I'll just go out to his paddock and check on him and call you back.'

Bill was snoozing in the sun on his deck chair with Bro at his feet. The dog was keeping watch, with one eye open and he let out a sound halfway between a growl and a friendly woof to warn his owner that someone had arrived.

'Is Mr Binks OK to ride?' Becky asked as Bill yawned into waking.

He nodded. 'Yes, he's absolutely fine. I had a little canter on him this morning — that cow dung worked a treat. And come down here to meet me tomorrow afternoon, girlie, because Queenie and Princess are ready for me to start training them.' Then pushing his bush hat over his eyes, Bill closed his eyes and went back to sleep.

Funny that he could remember the horses' names but not hers, Becky thought ruefully. Oh well, it didn't matter, the main thing was that Binky was fine to ride again. Cow dung? She'd never heard of it as a remedy for a foot infection before, but she would pass the information on to anyone at the pony club who was interested.

An hour later Becky and Megan were tearing along the

sand together with Pixie and Binky, both girls shrieking and laughing, free from schoolbooks, uniforms and homework for two whole weeks.

She knew she was asking a silly question, but Becky couldn't keep her amazing news from her friend any longer. 'Megan, seriously, can you keep a secret? Promise not to tell anyone — yet!'

'Yes, of course I can.' Megan was all ears.

'I've got a new pony. In fact I've got two new ponies, they're a mother and daughter — and they're Kaimanawas from the Central Plateau!'

'*Wowee*!' Megan reined Pixie to a halt. 'Let's take the ponies under the pohutukawa trees over there for a break and you can tell me all about it. You sly dog!'

After they had tethered their ponies to a large low branch of the nearest pohutukawa tree to rest, the two friends flopped down on the sand in the shade.

It had all started with the big mortgage on their farm earlier in the year and the fact that Binky was getting old, Becky explained. 'I saw an ad in the Horses for Sale section of the paper, saying that some Kaimanawa horses were being mustered for the first time and would be going really cheaply. The advertisement said they were great horses to ride and would be perfect for kids, and they put the date they would go up for sale.

'I cut out the ad, showed it to Mum and Dad and when I finally got them to agree, we drove down to look at them at the sale a couple of weekends ago. We were only going to get the one I'd chosen — you'll love her because she's a real darling with four little white socks, two more than Binky — then I heard they were going to kill her mare because the man said no one would want to have her because she was too old. I couldn't stand the thought of that so I said I'd buy her for fifty dollars out of my savings. That's why I have to clean out the milking shed every afternoon, as part of a deal I made with Dad so he would let me keep her.'

Megan leaned over and gently punched Becky's arm. 'Softy! That's a really kind thing to do — I'm sure we'll be able to find a way to use her too. Maybe someone at the pony club might need her.'

'No, I'm never, ever giving her up,' Becky protested. 'My baby has got enough to learn about in her new life without losing her mum as well. I've called my pony Kaimanawa Princess and then Mum came up with the bright idea of calling her mother Queenie.'

Now came the hard bit. Why hadn't she told Megan sooner? Becky explained, 'Megs, I couldn't tell you or anyone because they haven't been broken in yet and if the word got out, people like Danielle would be so snobby and catty about me having a cheap Kaimanawa pony.

'No one knows about them yet as pony club horses, but we've got a kind of unusual man staying at our place right now who says they're brilliant horses to ride and for showjumping. He's a real expert at breaking them in and we start on that at home tomorrow afternoon!

'There — you're the first to know.' Well, actually she was the second if she counted Rachel, but Rachel was a town girl who didn't ride or even know Megan. 'I can't wait to be able to ride my little Princess!'

'Are they the horses you see the signs about avoiding on the Desert Road?' Becky nodded and Megan burst out, 'Let me come and watch! I can't wait to see them and—' she broke off mid-sentence. 'What's that noise?'

The girls scrambled to their feet and followed the direction of the faint sounds. Wedged in the bank beside the trees, they saw a squirming sack tied at the top. 'Grab a sharp shell so we can cut it open,' Becky said.

Working furiously to a chorus of muffled mewing sounds, the girls ripped and tore at the sack until they managed to wedge open a large hole.

'Oh my goodness!' Megan's expression was one of total shock. 'How can people be so horrible and cruel? These poor little babies . . .' They stared down into the interior of the dirty bag and gently lifted out three tiny tabby and ginger kittens. The kittens wobbled unsteadily on the sand and blinked in the unaccustomed sunlight.

'At least they're still alive.' Becky felt the tears pouring down her cheeks. 'Aren't they gorgeous? Look, they've all still got big blue eyes! We were meant to be here today, Megs, to rescue them. Goodness knows how long they've been here. Your place is closest — we'd better get some milk into them quickly. This little ginger one looks so weak, it can hardly stand up on its little paws.'

The two girls stuffed the tiny kittens down their T-shirts to keep them warm and safe then, untying their horses, they headed for home.

Rather to her daughter's surprise, Megan's mother was as emotional as the girls had been when they first saw the kittens. 'Poor little pets,' she crooned at the two tiny tabby bodies, safely enclosed in her large arms. 'They're too small to drink from a saucer and probably don't even know how to. How can people be so terrible to animals?

'Megan, go to the bathroom and fetch the eye dropper from the top drawer. We'll have to feed them by hand until they can drink for themselves.'

'Does that mean we can keep them?' Megan asked hopefully.

'Why not? Since old Marmalade died, we've needed a farm cat or two to clear out any rats and mice from the barn. Anyway, they'll be good friends for each other,' she said, as the tabby pair began boxing each other in her arms.

'Megan, hop into the bedroom and bring out that shoe-box in my wardrobe. We'll cut the sides down and put in a soft towel so they have someplace to feel safe and begin to call home.'

That just left the frail ginger kitten to find somewhere to live. 'I'll give it to my little sister, Stephanie,' Becky volunteered. 'She's not into horses, but she's always wanted a cat. If this little baby has the strength to survive, that is . . .'

One dropper of milk later, Becky gently placed the wriggling orange bundle back inside her T-shirt and promised she would see Megan at home the following afternoon, so that she could meet Kaimanawa Princess and Queenie.

It felt quite strange in a nice kind of way, clip-clopping along the country road with a warm and furry, squiggling, squirming body kneading at her stomach. 'Steph! Steph!' There was no time to put Binky in his paddock so Becky tied him to the garden fence and rushed inside to find her sister.

'I've got a present for you. Hold out your hands and close your eyes tight!' Stephanie obediently did as she was told.

'Oooh! Wowee! Thank you!' She opened her eyes. 'What a beautiful kitten, is it really mine? That's the best present I've ever had!'

'Yeah, but first we'd better get Mum's OK on this,' Becky said nervously. 'She might go spare about another new animal so soon after the ponies.'

Stephanie screwed up her face. 'No, she wouldn't be so mean. This is going to be my very own little cat who's got red hair just like me and who'll sleep with me on my bed every single night. I'm going to call this little sweetheart Fluffybum!'

'It's probably a him as he's a ginger.' Toni Mitchell had caught the end of the conversation as she walked into the hall and glanced down at her daughter's cupped hands. 'Look Stephanie, I'm not going to argue with you about this. You can keep him, but the same rules apply as they do for Becky's ponies. You'll be responsible for looking after him and that includes feeding and cleaning up after him until he's house-trained.

'Dad and I will pay the vet's fees and his neutering

costs as soon as he's old enough.' She smiled. 'Didn't you girls know I like cats?'

'What about me?' Tim came roaring out of his bedroom. 'Becky's got two horses and now Steph's got a kitten. I want a farm bike!'

'If you can buy one for $100 or less, which is what the horses have cost us, then you can have one,' his mother replied reasonably.

What a great afternoon this had been. Becky ran out to put Mr Binks back in the paddock and stopped dead in her tracks. Ummm . . . Binky looked very pleased with himself with the remains of a plant dangling from the side of his mouth. Her mother's pride and joy, her beautiful front garden flowerbed, was no more.

Best to let her discover that for herself tomorrow.

'Megs, this afternoon come straight to the paddock about midday.' Becky decided it would be wise to give her friend advance warning. 'I'll meet you over there. Stephanie adores her new kitten but Mum's really wild with me and poor old Binky. I was so excited about the kitten I tethered him up to the front fence when I rushed in to find Steph.

'While I was inside, Binky ate up all Mum's plants and flowers and she's really on the warpath, so I'm keeping a low profile for the next day or two! Don't laugh, Megs — it's not funny. Well, it is a bit — you should have seen his happy face, but don't ever, ever let Mum know you think it is! See you then. Bye.'

When Megan arrived she tethered Pixie out of sight, then the two girls stood outside the Kaimanawas' paddock — at the distance Bill had ordered — to watch the action.

To their amazement and Becky's horror, Bill had sauntered up with a large stock-whip. Seeing their dismay, he hurried to reassure the girls. 'I always use them for breaking in horses, but I would never, ever hit them with it. You don't see stock-whips used here to round up horses but I used them all the time in Australia for breaking in camels and horses. You have to teach a horse to face up — a crack of the stock-whip and the horse comes up to you just like a dog coming to heel. A horse is an extremely sensitive animal, and very intelligent.

'A horse can understand what you're saying in two minutes as long as you've got them totally relaxed. Then you can tie a rope on them. But I won't be using the stock-whip for the first couple of sessions, which are just to get them familiar with me. Now watch what I'm doing and not a word or a gesture from either of you!'

Watched cautiously by Princess and Queenie, Bill stood outside the horses' yard looking so relaxed he was almost slumped over the rails. At the same time he was breathing steadily and slowly through his nose. He kept holding his breath almost to the point of fainting and then he broke eye contact with the horses.

Using an imaginary clock face, each time he would

slowly step out at about the 4 o'clock to 5 o'clock position from the horses, look at them and make eye contact. That was it for now. He wandered back to the girls. 'Come back in four hours for our next session, which you'll find more interesting.

'When most people go to break in a horse they stride into the yard, chests puffed out because of adrenaline, nerves or something like that, which frightens the horse. I don't operate that way.

'But if you're coming back, keep your distance like now and not a sound from either of you. And keep that horse of yours well out of sight,' he said sternly to Megan, who blushed scarlet. How on earth had he seen them arrive? She had been so careful. Bill must have eyes in the back of his head.

Four hours later, the girls watched in fascination as Bill slowly re-entered the paddock, making no attempt to approach the horses. He seemed happy just to stand there as relaxed as before and in a slumped position, breathing slowly through his nose.

He kept breathing down his nose until he was almost against the rail, then using his 'clock method' he moved to the 7 o'clock to 8 o'clock position in three slow steps, keeping eye contact but not threatening them in any way.

Then he breathed down his nose again — not hard — and when he was at the point of fainting, he breathed in again and took another three steps. The horses didn't move. Bill reached the rails on the other side of the yard part of the paddock and rested up, leaning against the rails for a smoke before walking slowly out of the gate.

He repeated the performance five minutes later, again maintaining his eye contact with the horses. This time he came back at about 8 o'clock on his 'clock' to where the horses were standing and walked slowly to the 1 o'clock mark.

As he had before, Bill breathed down his nose as he made eye contact, this time slowly walking towards them while allowing them the time and room to walk away.

Then he stepped outside the paddock again. By this time, he knew he'd won their trust — they had an escape route from him and they knew they didn't have to panic or charge him. Their minds had been put at rest.

That was it for the day, he told the two girls.

'I've never seen horses broken in like that before,' Megan ventured.

'No you probably haven't,' Bill agreed. 'But I'll have them both eating out of my hands by tomorrow afternoon and with some trust in humans. They'll be a piece of cake to ride in future.

'Remember, in the horses' eyes you're a predator, maybe they've never seen the bloke who's breaking them in before. They'll be spooked because they're away from their family herd and their own ground in the tussock lands. They'll be suffering from flight syndrome, which is the urge to run away from any potential danger. If you come bustling in determined to stamp your mark, in the horses' eyes you're the enemy. You've come in with a knife and fork as far as they are concerned.'

Becky and Megan were hanging on his every word.

'If you do what I've just shown you, you've removed two of their greatest fears. If you show the horses you're relaxed they won't be uptight. Look to get the horse to bond with you, then do it correctly.'

'What will happen next?' Megan asked, fascinated to see how Bill planned to break in the two wild ponies. The two girls listened carefully as he outlined his plans.

The next day he would lasso each of the ponies, throwing a rope over their heads and lead Queenie back to the shed, while he concentrated his energies on Princess, he told them. 'With the stock-whip, I'll flick the ground near her hooves. I learned this when I was working with camels, kicking up the dirt or sand to hurry him up and make him go quicker.

'I'll stand in the middle of the yard part of the paddock with a stock-whip and use the whip to almost touch her hooves. That'll block her from running around in circles. This time I won't look into her eyes, I'll look behind her shoulder area or half turn and go back the other way. I'll loop the rope into a noose and then move her by twisting my weight, never pulling her.'

It was all a matter of equal minds and mutual respect. Bill gave Becky one of his rare smiles. 'Never be frightened of her. Never let her turn back. All you're doing is trying to get her to face up. It's a piece of cake, girlie.'

Chapter 4

'It'll bring good luck'

A month had passed and Bill had long departed, leaving the farm as abruptly as he arrived. 'Well, that's it, folks, thanks for the company. Job done. You've got a couple of nice horses there and they'll do you well.'

How would they keep in touch, Becky demanded? 'I want you to share in their success when it happens, and I'm sure it will. It's been the most awesome experience watching you with them . . .'

Bill grinned and ruffled her hair. 'Like you did last time, just call up my mate, Paul, when you need to and he'll keep me posted with your news. We'll meet again some day, girlie, trust me.'

It really had been the most awesome experience,

Becky reflected. As Bill had predicted, both Princess and Queenie were eating out of his hands by the following day and when he introduced them to the saddle and bridle, they both took to them easily, as though they had been born to it.

Becky rode Princess while Bill preferred to gallop around on Queenie. 'This old girl's still got plenty of life left in her,' he would smile approvingly, giving the mare's neck a pat. 'Don't leave her standing around in the paddock all day, girlie — she's spent her life running around the mountains and she's used to lots of activity, just like the filly. I know you want to compete with Princess and that's a good call, but think about it. Queenie is too good a horse to waste.'

Princess excelled in jumping, clearing with ease the hurdles Bill placed strategically around the paddock. That excited Becky. Going over the hurdles with Mr Binks had been her passion at pony club.

Becky had a good seat, Bill said, and she also had the advantage of courage and spirit on a horse. 'You're a very good young horsewoman and I'm sure you already know the way to become a real top riding team is for you and your pony to understand each other instinctively, so that you face every jumping and riding challenge as one. And remember, Becky,' — ah, he did know her name, Becky noted happily — 'you're the one in control. Never doubt it because you don't want her to develop bad habits when you're presenting her at the fence and you have to hold your position so she can jump freely and comfortably.'

To start their programme, they had lined up three jumps with six stands and a dozen poles from the Jacksons' place as well as their own old ones. Under Bill's beady eye, Becky walked her horse over the pole, allowing Princess to stretch her head and neck down to look at it.

'Good stuff!' Bill grinned as the nosey Princess had a good look then progressed to a trot. 'OK. Next step, we'll jack ourselves up a little course in the centre of the paddock for you to trot around, always going straight before you approach at right angles to the centre of each pole . . . the real fun of jumping comes from riding the course, not just going over one jump again and again. That's boring stuff.'

Instead he urged her to vary the distance of the gaps, keep the pony's head and neck lowered over the poles and always maintain a steady contact with her hand and leg. 'It's hard work for a little pony to pick up all this stuff,' Bill said as he wound up the session for the day. 'Give her a piece of carrot, because it's time for her to have a good rest. I'll see you tomorrow!'

Soon they were galloping around the paddock as though they'd been together for years and in no time at all Kaimanawa Princess was eager for each new jumping challenge, showing an impressive turn of pace in the approach, take-off, flight and landing — and then rounding off her performance with a sassy show-off toss of her mane, a snort and flick of her tail.

Their confidence and steadiness grew, until the day Bill told Becky that they no longer needed him. 'I've got to head down the line to my mate's place for a while and old Bro is getting a bit bored hanging around in the bus all day.

'Give your pony club lady a call and tell her what you've got sitting out here on your farm. You're just about good enough to take it from there on your own, but you'll do better if you get her alongside with your plans for this little character.'

And then he stopped. 'Look, it's none of my business, girlie, but ask her to come on out and have a nosey at both of these Kaimanawa horses. No one's up with the play with them in the horse and pony club world yet, because this group is the first and maybe the only one to have come out of the wild, but I'm sure she'll like the look of Queenie, too.

'I'd buy her myself if I had a place of me own.' Then looking at Becky's upset expression, he added quickly, 'Not that I'd ever want to take her off you. It's a real nice feeling to see that mum and her daughter grazing happily together in the paddock. They've adjusted to their new lifestyle like real troopers. If they've got to be taken out of their own home range in the mountains, this is as good as it's going to get for them.'

Then, looking serious, he had a last word to his young

friend. 'I've brought you something to keep, Becky. It's not worth any money, but keep it because it will always remind you of where your ponies have come from and what they truly are.' Bill reached into his jeans pocket and fished out a small sheaf of tussock grass tied together with a piece of string. 'This is from the Argo Valley in the tussock lands where these two used to live. I called in there on my way here and gathered it for you.

'Always keep this little piece of tussock grass by your side when you're riding or if you need it for some reason to protect the horses. Know that it will bring good luck to you and your Kaimanawa Princess.'

Rachel was waiting for her by the school gates on the first morning of term and one look at her face was enough for Becky to ask nervously, 'What's gone wrong, Rach?'

'It's finally happened.' Rachel was choking out the words, her eyes brimming with tears. 'A couple of days ago when we were at the shops with Dad, Mum left a note on the kitchen table saying she was off and going to live in Auckland and that she'll be in touch when she finds somewhere to live.

'I don't even know where she is or how I can contact her . . . I miss her so much.' Rachel's voice had risen to a desolate wail.

Becky dropped her schoolbag and hugged Rachel, trying to think of what she could say or do to comfort her friend. Ignoring the curious stares from the other pupils coming through the gates, she said, 'Hey, it'll be all right, I'll help you. How's your dad handling things?'

Rachel wiped her eyes and said her dad was being pretty good really. 'He rang Nana, who lives alone in Thames since Grandad died, and from next week she's coming to live with us. Nana's quite bossy but she's a really good cook and Dad reckons she'll have all of us and the place ticking over in no time.

'So I suppose that's something, but she's not my mum — and it's my birthday on Saturday. What a stinking, horrible birthday present . . . no party, no cake, no Mum, probably no presents as I know Dad won't remember — no nothing!'

'Come and stay with us for the weekend,' Becky insisted. 'Dad could pick you up on Saturday afternoon after the milking, I'll ask Mum to make you a birthday cake and we'll have a really good time.

'You can meet my Kaimanawa horses and our cute little Fluffybum, Steph's new ginger kitten who's really naughty but so cute. He hides behind doors and then springs out to ambush us as we walk down the hall. I'll tell you the amazing way he came into our lives . . .' Rachel was smiling. That was better. Arm in arm the two friends walked into the classroom.

Yes, Rachel was welcome to stay for the weekend, Toni said that evening and she would bake a chocolate cake with twelve candles, for a birthday meal on Saturday night. 'She can sleep on the camp stretcher in your room,

Becky. I'll buy her a big box of chocolates from us when I go to the supermarket later this week. Poor kid.'

For some reason, Bill Worth's words flashed through Becky's mind. 'Get in touch with your pony club instructor and ask her to come out to the farm and meet your ponies. Get her on side . . .'

Flicking through the directory at the back of her pony club manual, Becky saw Julia Williams's name and phone number. She picked up the phone and her instructor answered on the third ring. 'Yes? Hello, Becky Mitchell! How are things going with you?'

Well, actually very well, and she had a lot to tell her if Mrs Williams had the time to listen.

'Yes, of course. I'm all ears!' she replied.

'It all sounds very interesting,' Julia Williams said when Becky finally ended her tale. 'I knew a few Kaimanawa ponies were coming onto the horse market, but I've never had any direct contact with them or even seen them in the show ring. And Mr Bill Worth sounds an interesting kind of character.'

She would drive out that Saturday afternoon to meet Princess and Queenie and she would be wearing her riding gear as Becky should as well, to put the two horses through their paces in the paddock.

'We'll see if they're as good as you say they are, Becky,' she said. 'The arrival of your Kaimanawa Princess will

certainly give everyone a big surprise at pony club —
maybe the local paper will be interested, as it'll certainly
be a first for us, and most other pony clubs for that matter.'
And then she paused. 'I've just had a thought about your
Queenie — I wonder if she could be suitable for helping
disabled and disadvantaged children?

'We've been contacted by a group who are looking for
horses that might be suitable for children who are disabled
or emotionally troubled, because apparently contact with
a horse does wonderful things for their self-confidence.

'I said at the time that we didn't have any horses at the
club that would fit the bill . . . but, who knows? If she's
docile enough perhaps we could borrow Queenie and
bring her to the pony club to help these young people.'

It must have been her week for bright ideas, Becky thought
as she and Princess cruised over a jump the following
afternoon. How about giving Rachel the kind of birthday
present Becky knew she longed for more than anything
else? She knew her friend had always wanted to ride but
couldn't afford to because their family was so hard up.

How would it be if — in exchange for giving the pony
club free access to Queenie — she could get Mrs Kingi
or Mrs Williams to give Rachel free riding lessons? But
lessons were just the start of the costs involved with a
horse, as her parents kept reminding her.

She would run over to the Jacksons' the next day and
ask Tom for that saddle and tack he'd promised her.
Rachel was smaller than she was so she could wear her

old jodhpurs and her old hard hat. While it had certainly seen better days it was still perfectly sound, but she hadn't used it since her grandparents had given her a new one for Christmas. It wasn't up to scratch for competing, but it would be OK for learning to ride — and while she was learning it was quite acceptable for her to wear gumboots instead of boots.

If Rachel really liked riding and pony club, her nana could knit her a vest in the club colours. Brilliant!

Becky was surprised to see Mrs Williams had someone sitting beside her in the Land Rover's passenger seat when she pulled up at the Mitchells' front door early on Saturday afternoon.

'Becky, this is Gina Parker from the group I was telling you about,' Julia Williams explained. 'I hope you don't mind but I gave her a call after you spoke to me the other night and she's very interested in seeing Queenie, so I decided the best idea would be to bring her out today. Now, lead the way!'

Becky had spent more than an hour grooming both horses before her visitors arrived and their once shaggy coats and long dreadlocks had given way to glossy coats and shiny manes.

Binky had been an interested spectator from his side of the paddock, watching the swish-swish of Becky's brushing movement as first one, then the other horse

submitted to the treatment. 'There! You look beautiful —
now remember to behave and I'll give both of you some
nice juicy carrot and apple pieces after my instructor's
gone home.' Becky planted a parting kiss on each pony's
nose.

Julia Williams cast an expert eye over the two ponies as
they stood alongside each other under the shade of one of
the trees that ringed the eastern end of the paddock. The
jumps were in place, the sun was shining — now it was
up to pony and rider to show what they could do.

Both ponies were fairly small, stocky and sturdy rather
than handsome but on the plus side they were in good
condition, their ears were pricked in anticipation and the
spirit in their eyes showed up as bright and intelligent —
particularly for the little filly. Julia ticked off the credits
in her mind. 'Right, Becky. Off you go on Kaimanawa
Princess — let me see you two go over the jumps and
around the course you've set up.'

Did Princess sense how important this was? Becky
wondered to herself. She had never jumped better or more
confidently, neatly tucking in her legs before each jump
and flying over every hurdle with the greatest of ease.

'That was certainly impressive.' Julia Williams beamed
as Becky cantered up to her instructor. 'And you've only
been riding her for a couple of months. Amazing. There's
a lot of work still to be done,' she added hastily 'but
when the pony club reopens for the season I'll certainly
look forward to working with you both. We might even

produce our first New Zealand Kaimanawa champion.

'Now dismount and tie her up to the fence rail because I want to have a ride on Queenie and I want my friend Gina to give her opinion. By the way, what are you doing with Mr Binks these days? I see him over there watching the action with great attention.'

Becky told Mrs Williams she was still giving Binky the odd gallop, but like Queenie he wasn't lined up for anything special.

Mrs Williams replied that the reason why she was asking was that he had always had a gentle nature and Gina had mentioned that it would be great for her group if they had two horses they could work with.

Mr Binks would be a natural for the job — what they called a real 'schoolmaster' in pony club circles. Most young riders started under the care of a 'schoolmaster' horse, as Becky had when she was seven — good solid ponies like Mr Binks that were great for children who were learning to ride. Ponies who could still perform well, even if their young riders were still learning their basic riding skills.

They were ponies and horses who knew the ropes — they'd been there, done that, weren't scared of things like tractors, cars or trains and were absolutely perfect for disabled children, happy just to plod along and do what they were told. Of course, Mr Binks deserved retirement, but Julia felt sure that as well as spending his days grazing in the paddock, the old chestnut would love having young children back in his life again.

'Righto, Queenie, I'm going to take you around the paddock at a gentle walk, then we'll stop and then we'll trot and then we'll stop. I'll know her temperament by the end of that time. Keep an eye out, Gina.' With a swing into the saddle, Julia Williams and Queenie set off.

Twenty minutes later, Julia Williams reined Queenie in, with a huge smile on her face. She would be ideal for their needs and, on Julia's strong recommendation, so would Mr Binks.

Gina explained some more about the riding programme. 'Some of the children we deal with have never had an animal, let alone a horse, so they're really scared of them. That's why we need pony-sized horses, and although Mr Binks may be rather big, we can use him to show the kids how to care for a horse, which is also great therapy.

'We work with young people aged between eleven and thirteen because it's easier for them to understand what's going on and they can tell us what they feel,' she continued.

'One boy we had at another centre was so frightened of horses he wouldn't go near them, but then he conquered his fear and was so proud of himself, telling his grandmother later that he could whisper in the horse's ear and he'd do what he wanted him to do. It was a great confidence booster. So yes, if you and your parents are happy about it, we'd love to have both Queenie and Mr Binks come to pony club on our special days to help our special group of young people,' Gina said.

With her heart racing, Becky faced the two women and laid down her terms. She'd never done anything like this before, but this was for her friend Rachel. 'That's fine with us, I've talked it over with Mum and Dad and there's no cost involved however you want to use them. But there is one condition. My friend Rachel's mother has left their family and she's finding it very hard at the moment. Her family is really short of money, so in return for the use of my ponies, I'd like Rachel to have free riding lessons on Queenie and free membership of the pony club.'

The two women exchanged a look.

'It's Rachel's birthday today,' Becky continued nervously, 'and Mum's invited her to stay the night with us and she's baked her a cake as well. I'd love to be able to offer her this as the best birthday present in the whole world.'

Gina grinned. 'How could we turn down such a moving request? If that's all right with the pony club, we're happy to donate the hire fee from the horses towards teaching your friend to ride.'

Julia Williams smiled broadly. 'Yes, that's absolutely fine with me and I'll speak to Marg Kingi tonight so we can start Rachel's riding lessons as soon as pony club resumes. I think we could be in for a very interesting season, Becky. See you next week.'

In the meantime, Bruce had collected Rachel from her house. As soon as she arrived at the farm she ran out to the horse paddock to see her friend, arriving just as the two women were leaving. '*Ooooh*. Aren't they gorgeous? So cute!' She beamed as she saw the horses. 'Would I be allowed to stroke them?'

'Of course and I can promise you something even better,' Becky grinned, reaching into her rucksack. 'Just lay the palm of your hand as flat as you can and then I'll put a piece of carrot on it. Don't pull away. They won't bite you, and you can feed them as well as stroking them.'

Princess ambled over to Becky, while, treading delicately and hesitantly, Queenie walked towards Rachel and lowered her head to accept the carrot offering. 'Oh, she's so beautiful,' Rachel gushed. 'I only wish . . .' and then she stopped, turning her head away so Becky couldn't see the silly tears that were threatening to fall down her cheeks.

I know what you wish and just you wait until tonight! Becky thought to herself. She grabbed the rucksack and after hosing each horse down and placing their covers on their backs, said, 'Time to go home.'

'Happy birthday, dear Rachel,' the family sang as Toni brought in the cake with twelve candles blazing. 'Make a wish!' Would she be allowed to make two while blowing out her candles, Rachel asked timidly?

'Yes, because you're a guest you're allowed two — that's our new family tradition from now on,' Tim said, winking at his parents.

Rachel's eyes were closed and this was taking for ever. Stephanie was about to object when she got a sharp jab in the ribs from her sister. 'Shut up, Steph,' Becky mouthed.

Ta-raa! Presents! The biggest box of chocolates she had ever received and then, 'Close your eyes again, Rach. Tim, come with me,' Becky ordered.

A moment later Tim yelled, 'You can open them now!' as he pretended to stagger into the room carrying a saddle and tack while Becky followed with her jodhpurs and helmet. 'These are all yours, Rachel, and I've done a deal for you to have free riding lessons on Queenie, and membership of our pony club, starting from next week. You can ride over on your bike and they'll look after everything for you.

'All you need now for learning to ride are some T-shirts, your gumboots and — when you join the club — get your nana to knit you a vest in the club colours.'

It had been the most perfect night of her life. Rachel hugged each member of the Mitchell family in turn. 'I'll never forget it and I won't let you down. Riding lessons on Queenie — that's one of my wishes come true already!'

Watching her friend sleeping peacefully alongside her, Becky looked up at the ceiling late that night. It had been great to see Rachel so happy. So why was she feeling so sick in the pit of her stomach — why oh why had this happened on today of all days to cast a great cloud over her happiness?

It had been a chance remark by Mrs Williams as they were about to leave and perhaps she got it wrong. 'Funny that you should have rung me about the Kaimanawa horses this week, Becky, because after your call I did some checking up on them.

'I've heard a horrible rumour, and mind you it's only a rumour, that there's a plan to kill most, if not all, of the Kaimanawa horses.

'They're going to muster them up in the hills and drive them down to the plains of the Central Plateau and shoot them, all because some people are calling them vermin and want them removed from the Kaimanawas. After seeing your lovely horses this afternoon, I can only hope I'm wrong . . .'

Her beautiful precious Princess and Queenie vermin? With her heart thudding, Becky was too shocked to reply. But what on earth could she do to help save them?

Reaching into the top drawer of her dressing table, Becky's hands strayed about until she felt a small clump of tussock grass, which she removed and clasped between her hands. 'Please God, please save the Kaimanawa horses,' she prayed.

Chapter 5

'We'll show them!'

The arrival of the Mitchells' horse float on the opening day of the new season was sensation enough, as everyone knew Mr Binks was retired and thought Becky had no other horse. But when the float was parked up and its back door unbolted, surprise turned to amazement as Becky emerged with a small, stocky black horse with legs carefully bandaged, who didn't look like anything anyone had seen before at the pony club.

'What is *that*?' Trust rude Danielle. She was openly sneering at Princess, and as always happened when Becky was confronted by Danielle, she felt the blood rising in her face. 'She's my beautiful Kaimanawa pony and she's come from the Central Plateau.'

The questions poured out thick and fast.

'What's her name?' from Becky's friend Suzy. 'Where did you get her? She looks so sweet. Isn't she too small to jump over the big hurdles?'

And from Jo, 'Oh my gosh, I can't believe she came out of the Kaimanawas!'

Well she did and what's more, her mare Queenie was going to be a part of the pony club scene in future, Becky told them. 'Kaimanawa Princess is a fast learner and I'll be riding her on the flat and over the jumps.'

'Aren't these Kaimanawas the wild horses some idiots want rounded up and slaughtered?' the club's champion male rider Ross Edwards asked. 'I read something about them in the pony club gazette.' Becky looked away without replying. She didn't want any reminder of what Mrs Williams had told her, and was still desperately hoping it wasn't true.

Automatically Becky reached towards Kaimanawa Princess's saddle blanket, onto which she had stitched a small outside pocket and dome, and touched it to bring good luck. Becky had decided to follow Bill's advice to the letter, and take his little clump of tussock grass wherever Princess went.

Inside that pocket on the blanket under her saddle was the safest place to keep her tussock grass and no one would know what the pocket held or what it meant. But if she thought her quiet little action had gone unnoticed, she was wrong.

And now for the second shock of the morning. It was

Queenie's turn to be unloaded — a dark bay pony, clearly older but not much larger than the filly who had led the way from the float. There was more comment and more explanations.

'Queenie is coming to help my friend Rachel, who's learning to ride and she'll also be here on a regular basis with Mr Binks, working with young people who have physical or emotional challenges,' Becky announced importantly.

In the background by the secretary's caravan, she could see Rachel standing alone and looking awkward but excited. Rachel recognised some of this horsey set from intermediate school but to start learning from the beginning, at the age of twelve, when all of the others in the club were obviously skilled riders was — Rachel had to face it — really embarrassing. Rachel hoped her first lesson with Queenie could take place well out of the public view.

She needn't have worried. Marg Kingi, a kindly woman, guessing who the newcomer was, bustled over and introduced herself. 'Hello, you're Rachel, right? I'm going to be your instructor. I believe your saddle and bridle are in Becky's float. Go over and collect them, along with your horse and meet me over in that far corner in ten minutes. I saw your horse being unloaded — she looks nice and friendly and I'm certain we'll turn you into a rider in no time at all.'

There was also a seven-year-old boy and a girl of eight who were starting in their group that day, she told

Rachel. 'Don't be worried about the fact that you're older than they are, they'll be terribly proud to know they're learning alongside a big girl and you'll probably have two devoted little followers.'

Rachel set off for the float, willing Becky to be there. Otherwise how on earth was she going to stick a bridle on Queenie and then to lead her over on her own, when she didn't have a clue what to do?

To her relief, she saw Becky standing by the float with Queenie saddled up and ready to go. 'I'll walk over with you, but you can lead her, Rach. Good practice.'

What a buzz, leading Queenie on her own with Becky striding along beside her and before that to hear Mrs Kingi say 'your horse' — she wasn't, of course, but it was nice to daydream.

Rachel and the two young riders called Todd and Courtney stood in a semicircle with their ponies as Mrs Kingi outlined what they were to do. 'Today I'll show you the first steps in learning how to care for your pony and to give you some knowledge about horses.

'For example, you mount a horse on the left because way back in history, soldiers carried their swords on the left so they had to mount on that side and we've done it that way ever since. We'll have some mounting practice, then I'll show you how to sit in the saddle with your back straight and after that we'll have a little riding — today will be at walking pace.

'And, always remember, horses are herd animals who don't like being on their own. If your pony doesn't live with other horses make sure there are other animals like goats, cattle or sheep nearby or sharing the paddock. Your pony will like to have your company, too — so even if you're not riding, don't forget to visit and talk to them and, most importantly, give them lots of affection and pats.'

Over in the main area, the club riders had their horses lined up for inspection — grooming and gear checks by the instructors, followed by some flat work. Becky couldn't help but feel anxious. On her very first outing, Kaimanawa Princess was expected to trot in circles with other skilful and practised horses like Pixie, Rajah and Proud Basil.

'We need to see some improvement here.' Mrs Williams frowned as Becky and her horse ended their segment of work. 'We've got a lot of work ahead of us.'

Just let them wait till the jumping sessions this afternoon, Becky thought as she stroked her pony's neck and whispered 'We'll show them!'

Two hours later Rachel and Becky sat on the grass with their backs propped against the float, eating their packed lunches. 'How did it go?' Becky grinned.

'It was just the *best*. But it's quite hard to try and remember everything.' Rachel frowned. 'Would I be allowed to come over some time when it's not pony club to give Queenie a stroke and help you groom her? Mrs Kingi said it was good for them . . . I know she's yours but if it's OK I'd really want to because I do love her. And can I stay on until this afternoon to watch you and Kaimanawa Princess doing the jumps? This is so exciting! It almost makes up for everything else . . .'

Megan and Becky had their horses lined up for the early afternoon exercise round and, following that, the jumping course. Danielle on Rajah was as immaculate as ever doing the Cavalletti exercise with the small crossed poles, trotting through each hurdle as though horse and rider were as one.

'I can't stand her, but she is good,' Becky muttered crossly as the two friends watched Danielle's faultless exhibition.

'Look, matey, my Pixie's every bit as good as Rajah so don't let her spook you over Princess. Get out there and show everyone!' Megan gave her a friendly shove.

With her ears pricked forward Kaimanawa Princess advanced on the course, put in a 100 per cent performance on the Cavalletti exercise poles and then cleared the sequence of one-metre jumps without a falter. As they trotted back to the group Becky was astounded to hear the other riders cheering and clapping. 'Wow!' and 'What a star!'

Mrs Williams was all smiles as she came over to Becky and Princess. 'Well done, she's certainly a grand little jumper. When we tidy up the other work she needs to master and get her understanding what she has to do in the dressage, we may have a true champion.

'This has been a top introduction to the club, Kaimanawa Princess,' she said as she stroked the pony's nose. 'You've given everyone a good jumping lesson this afternoon — perhaps you might like to take over my job and teach those other horses a thing or two!'

Meanwhile, in Wellington an intense discussion on the future of Kaimanawa horses was taking place in a small government office close to Parliament.

'We have a real problem about getting rid of these wretched animals—' A member of the conservation lobby leaned across the table to confront one of the government representatives. '—and your lot in government can take a large part of the blame. In 1981 Kaimanawa horses became protected under New Zealand law. Because of that the horses were recognised by the United Nations as a breed of special significance and rarity and registered as a special herd.

'So not only do you have to change their protected status under New Zealand law, you'll have to lobby the United Nations to change their ruling — and to do that you need to prove they're not a special or significant herd.'

The spokesman was getting angrier with every sentence. 'You will be aware that since that protection notice was listed Kaimanawa horse numbers have multiplied and, in a landscape where some indigenous plant life dates back millions of years, they've become a menace. To those of us who care for the land and our native flora, the horses have to go. And we have the army on our side.

They regard them as nuisances — useful only as target practice, according to some of the officers at Waiouru Army Camp.'

The government officer shook his head, saying it wasn't quite so simple. 'First of all next year is election year and I don't expect that sort of action would go down very well with the public. For some reason New Zealanders love these horses.'

And it wasn't just New Zealanders who loved their wild horses, he said. There had been a similar reaction in the United States some years earlier when their wild horses had been threatened with similar action. Shuffling through the papers on his desk, he read from his notes:

'A Mustang is a free-roaming feral horse of the North American west descended from horses brought to the Americas by the Spanish. In 1971, a public outcry moved Congress to pass the Wild Free-Roaming Horse and Burro Act, granting federal protection to America's wild horses and burros as living symbols of the historic and pioneer spirit of the West, which continue to contribute to the diversity of life forms within the Nation and enrich the lives of the American people.'

Like the Kaimanawas, the Mustang herds could be traced back to lots of different origins. 'Some have a mix of ranch stock and more recent breed releases, while others are relatively unchanged from the original Iberian stock introduced by the Spanish, most strongly represented in the most isolated populations.'

He pushed his spectacles back up his forehead. 'And then there's the Maori factor to consider. Since the 1870s they've treasured their own Kaimanawa herds in the northern lands of the Central Plateau. I can't imagine how you could expect us to march onto Maori-owned land and take their horses off them to slaughter, without facing an almighty row.'

The translation of Kaimanawa means 'eat the wind' he explained. 'Maori mean by this that the brave must survive on their own resources — even when food is scarce and the future is in doubt, the brave will eat the wind and somehow endure. To them this is a fitting name for their wild horses, and they'll fight tooth and nail to protect them.'

The official ended the meeting, saying: 'I will speak with the Minister, but at this point in time, if you wish to have any chance of getting rid of these horses to save some tiny centimetre-high plants, however ancient they may be, I would suggest that you talk to no one of this meeting.'

Everyone's favourite highlight of the pony club year came in the middle of the summer school holidays when they all went to pony club camp for ten days at the Kingis' sheep farm down on the coast, about an hour out of town.

When she explained about the camp to Rachel, Becky said, 'We'll stick Queenie in the float with us to keep the costs right down. You've got to come! It's the best fun. Lots of parents come and help, we go trekking up in the hills, sleep in the shearers' huts, which are quite dungy but good fun because we all sleep together on mattresses on the floor.

'We have great beach races with the horses, we swim and have barbecues round a big fire every night. Mr Kingi plays the guitar and we all sing — it's just the most awesome time!'

'How much will it cost?' Rachel asked doubtfully.

'Not much, only about $100 I think . . .'

Rachel fell silent. Not much. $100. How would she manage to pull that one off? Spending ten days riding with Queenie and being with her new friends at pony club, especially Megan and Becky, was Rachel's idea of heaven. 'I'll try my best,' she promised. 'There's nothing I'd rather do for the holidays.'

'Well, you'd better hurry up and make up your mind because they can't take everyone and it's first in, first served.' Becky stood up. 'Come on, Rach, let's celebrate our last term at intermediate by having a race across the field!'

She would see if she could find work in the local supermarket, packing shelves after school. That should be worth something. No, she was far too young to be employed in any capacity, the deputy manager told Rachel as she presented herself at his office later that week.

'Look at you, you're still in intermediate school uniform! We'd get into serious trouble if we employed you. Come back again in a couple of years.'

Then she tried the local newspaper. She'd be the right age to be a paper girl and she did have a bike. Even if the pay wasn't much, by taking on a double round she knew she could just about make it.

But to her dismay even that door was closed. A friendly woman at the front desk said that while normally there would be no problem, 'we have no vacancies at present and there's even a waiting list for paper delivery jobs. Come back again in a couple of months dear, things might have improved then . . .'

She was good at ironing. Perhaps she could knock on doors and offer to take in people's ironing, to get that $100, but first she would ask Nana's advice — she'd understand.

Seeing her granddaughter's troubled face later that afternoon, Laura Montgomery suggested they have a cup of tea together while everyone else was out of the house.

It all tumbled out the wrong way. Rachel had intended to stay calm and to present her grandmother with her business plan for making that $100: 'I'll knock on doors or put flyers in letter boxes and collect their clothes before or after school.' Instead, she burst into tears and gabbled out: 'I want to go to pony club camp . . . more than anything . . . Queenie won't cost much . . .

everyone's going to be there but me . . .' and a wail to finish. 'Oh Nana, what can I do?'

Her grandmother said she could start by explaining what was bothering her slowly and carefully. But first she should drink her tea and eat some of the homemade biscuits that sat invitingly on the plate in front of her.

'Nana, I need $100 to go to the pony club camp for ten days in January.' There. She'd said it. Not so hard. 'How can I find the money? I've tried some places for work but I'm too young or there are no vacancies.'

'Is that all that's bothering you, dear?' Her grandmother smiled. 'Since I've been living with you I've got nothing much to spend my pension on, so I'll go down to the Post Office first thing tomorrow and withdraw that $100. Phone the pony club lady straight away and tell her you're on for the camp.'

Why had she ever thought her nana was an old boss? Rachel ran over to her grandmother and hugged her. Then she bent over and kissed her lined cheeks. 'Thank you so much, Nana. You don't know how much it means to me.'

'I think I do, dear, and I hope you have a lovely time.'

After the buzz of happiness she was feeling after she finished her call to the camp organiser, her good mood was clouded by a phone call from Auckland shortly afterwards. Rachel answered the call to hear her mother's bright voice at the other end.

'Hello, Rachel darling. I'm hoping you'll come up to stay for a couple of weeks in the middle of January and bring the younger children with you. You can look after them during the day while I'm out at work, but at the weekends we can go to the zoo or the movies, or the beach and we'll have a really good time together . . .'

While she had missed her mother so much, Rachel could hardly believe what she heard herself saying. 'Sorry, Mum, but I can't. I'm going to pony club camp then.'

There was silence on the line, and then Rachel heard her mother say she had never expected her to be so selfish, 'and that goes for your brother, too. I offered him the same chance and he's turned me down as well, saying he's starting his apprenticeship that week. I think they sound like a couple of excuses to avoid coming up here to be with me!'

Rachel knew that wasn't true. She was booked into camp and Glenn really was starting his building apprenticeship in January. Rachel took a deep breath. 'If you're talking about being selfish Mum, how about you leaving us to fend for ourselves without even saying goodbye? You broke my heart.'

A huge truck arrived at the pony club to load up the horses. Some families travelling alongside the truck, like the Mitchells, had brought their own floats to keep their costs down.

They were off to camp and Marg Kingi, at the centre

of the action, was issuing a volley of orders. 'Take your time leading the ponies on board please kids and make sure those leg bandages are secure. We don't want any horses injured before we even set off!'

It had to be the most beautiful setting in New Zealand — long, sweeping, white-gold, sandy beaches with gracious old pohutukawa trees laden with red Christmas flowers fringing the grass verges between road and beach. To the right of the road lay a steep curving drive up to the Kingis' property where sheep and cattle gazed curiously as first a horse truck and then several floats spilled out their contents of humans and horses onto the ground.

'You've got half an hour to unpack your sleeping bags and clothes in the shearers' huts up there — choose your own beds — and we'll all meet here in the drive for a cold drink followed by a short trek.

'Then we're off down to the beach for a swim,' Marg Kingi added. 'This is a holiday for the horses and for you, so the most important thing is to enjoy yourselves.'

Megan's mother was in charge of the roster for daily duties, and as usual, they wouldn't be tough or too time-consuming, their hostess added. 'If everyone does something each day, these duties, like peeling the potatoes, clearing the dishes or washing up, will take very little time.'

There was a tennis court they could use when they weren't riding, Megan pointed out to Rachel, and they could also go to the beach for a swim whenever they wanted, as long as there was a parent to supervise. 'And, for the last two years the musterers have let us join the sheep muster for a day. That's really exciting but you have to get up in the dark, at about five in the morning. It's really cool.'

The horses would live together in a huge paddock, she explained, which they seemed to like, but if one decided to take off, the others would probably follow, 'and then watch out, all hell breaks loose! C'mon, hurry up, Rach, find yourself a mattress and then we'll go off and join Becky.'

With Kaimanawa Princess and Queenie stepping across the steep terrain of the sheep station, the girls made their way back down to the drive for an orange drink before following Ross and Tara and the other horses who were heading for the nearby hills.

It turned out to be a camp of real surprises for Rachel. She had thought Danielle and Rajah, Jackie and Proud Basil would be at the forefront of every trek, even the muster, because they led the way at the pony club. But no. Their horses were so expensive and so precious, they were scared of letting them run free in the rugged hills, or competing in the helter-skelter of the beach races — to Rachel's amazement they made excuses to avoid the tough assignments, saying they preferred to relax on the farm or at the beach.

'Why come on a horse camp if you're not prepared to try everything?' she asked Jackie innocently one evening.

Trying not to explode with laughter, the other riders standing close by made themselves scarce.

'Oh, it's not that. I've got a cold and I don't feel well enough to do anything too hard. Proud Basil would love to take on the tough challenges, he's one of the bravest horses in the club. Maybe Danielle and I'll join you tomorrow,' Jackie replied crossly.

'Didn't you know?' Becky was still laughing when Rachel joined her later. 'Jackie and Danielle always find different excuses to duck the treks — of course they're scared of doing anything that might harm their expensive horses. If their horses got injured their parents would go absolutely ballistic!'

Then there were the beach races. As expected, Pixie and Princess were right up at the front as twenty-five riders hurtled along the beach, but who would have thought old Queenie would find a new wind?

Rachel was terrified as her horse gathered pace to take on horses like Tara, because she knew she wasn't good enough to handle this level of speed — she just prayed she could hang on until the front horses had stopped and Queenie had slowed down. But on the sixth night of the camp Queenie halted so abruptly Rachel was sent flying over her head.

Whew. She lay winded on the sand, with her pride in tatters as Marg Kingi raced over to her. 'Any bones broken? No, can't see anything. Get up right away, Rachel, and I'll go and grab that naughty Queenie. You're to climb straight back on her because she cannot be allowed to win this little power struggle!'

Rachel woke in the eerie first light of dawn on the second-to-last day and pulled on her jeans and sweater, then joined the musterers as they rode through the hills — their eye-dogs working furiously — rounding up the sheep to be brought down and shorn by the shearers who were due to move into the huts as the pony club moved out.

She watched each day as the two Kaimanawa horses stood out from all of the others, relishing the steep terrain and covering it as easily as a walk on the flat. Each night she sat with the others around the campfire with the warmth of the sun lingering on their faces, wolfing down chops, sausages, potatoes, salads, freshly caught fish and other seafood . . . listening and then joining in as Luke Kingi pulled out his guitar to play the latest hit songs. She sighed with happiness as she watched the sun setting on the horizon, throwing the mighty pohutukawas into dark relief against a blue-purple sea.

How could Rachel ever explain to her family all the experiences that had melded into one glorious whole? It had been, as Becky had promised, the most awesome holiday.

Chapter 6

A theft

It was exactly six months since Becky had introduced Kaimanawa Princess to the pony club and today was their first major public outing — at the annual Western Bay of Plenty Gymkhana, almost two hours' drive from the Mitchells' farm.

There had been so much for Kaimanawa Princess to learn and understand during those six months and in Julia Williams the pony found herself a staunch ally — the instructor handling the pony's high-spirited nature with patience and skill at every stumbling block she faced.

Added to that, there had been weeks of practice in the paddocks with Pixie and Kaimanawa Princess learning to work together on their entry for the Dual Jumps competition at the gymkhana.

That had been Megan's idea. The physical similarity in colouring of the two ponies, both black with white markings, would make them striking to look at as they combined with their riders over a series of jumps.

'Like one great black wave surging up and down with nice splashes of white,' Megan enthused. 'The judges will really like that . . . we've just got to make sure our pair are exactly in sync all the way. Let's wear the same-coloured gear for that event, Becks — navy blue jackets and white helmets. We'll wow them!'

Rachel too had progressed and could now ride — with far less skill but able to keep pace — with Becky and Megan at the weekends and in the holidays, which had her grinning from ear to ear. She would never be any better than average, she knew that, but to feel the joy of cantering along a deserted beach on Queenie with the mare's hooves pounding on the edge of the waves had opened up a new and exciting life.

And since upending Rachel in the beach race at camp Queenie had been goodness itself. 'Did you really intend to throw me off, you naughty old girl?' Rachel had asked her once. A wicked roll of the eye was her answer.

Rachel had asked to be allowed to come to the gymkhana to watch Becky and Princess compete and, riding out to the farm on her bike early that morning, she fussed over Queenie while Becky prepared Princess for the day ahead.

'Sorry, Queenie, we're not quite in that class.' She scratched the mare's chin affectionately. 'But, hey, I've brought you some yummy apple pieces which I'll give you as a reward after I've groomed your coat.'

Becky was entering the gymkhana along with the club's other leading riders, to compete for prize money in the flat classes, the jumping events and — her big ambition — to take out the show's ultimate reward, that of Champion Pony for the flat or jumping classes. That handsome broad purple champion's ribbon would look great pinned up in pride of place on her bedroom wall.

Kaimanawa Princess had been plaited and groomed as carefully as Mr Binks had been on his final pony club appearance and, although she felt disloyal in thinking it, Becky thought she looked even smarter.

Her gleaming jet black coat with its pattern of diamonds Becky had water-brushed onto her hind quarters — in exactly the same position as Megan planned to put the same pattern on Pixie — looked spectacular. But this time her mother's mascara stick stayed put in the bathroom cabinet. Princess had such long black lashes there was nothing more she needed to do.

A quick race inside for a shower and clean-up, then it was time to put on her riding gear for the show. A new navy riding jacket with her pony club badge pinned to one of its lapels, her best white shirt, club tie, cream jodhpurs and white helmet, with her hair tucked neatly into a hair net under the hard hat.

'You look pretty flash!' Rachel teased.

It was going to be a hot day and they arrived early so they could grab a cool shady spot under the trees.

Kaimanawa Princess was at her peak of fitness, and for the six events Becky had entered, she would need to be fit if she was to score well enough in each one to qualify for the Champion Pony classes.

Becky warmed Princess up for half an hour, then tied her alongside the other horses from the club before setting off with Megan to walk the course.

'Let's go around several times walking from the start to finish flags,' Megan suggested. 'If we want to win we've got to be smart-as and suss out the lines we need to take coming into the fences before we give Pixie and Princess a few practice jumps over one of the hurdles.'

On their return to the horses, and as she always did when she took her pony to the club, Becky reached for the pocket of the saddle blanket. This time, though, there was no little reassuring bump. Frantically she pulled open the dome of the pocket to see whether her lucky tussock grass had moved from its usual place.

It was gone. Becky flew across to the float and wrenched opened its back door. It had been there when they left home — could it have fallen on the floor? But that was impossible!

One look at the distraught girl with tears pouring down her cheeks was enough. Julia Williams interrupted her instructions to Ross Edwards and strode over to Becky. 'What on earth's the matter, why are you crying?'

Becky poured out the story of Bill's gift and why it meant so much to her. 'I never go to a pony club event without my little bundle of Kaimanawa tussock grass. It means everything to me . . .' and then she stopped, too choked with emotion to speak any more.

'Who else knew you keep this lucky grass in your saddle blanket?' her instructor asked in a sharp tone.

Only one or two people in the pony club, Becky said. 'But they're my best friends, they wouldn't take it.'

'Leave it with me,' Julia Williams ordered, 'and meanwhile pull yourself together, Becky. You can't ride in this state. Go now and wash your face — and remember, I want no gossip with anyone about what has happened.

'When I find your tussock grass, and I'm sure I will, it will be returned to you and I want no questions asked. This kind of thing can be very damaging within a club. Agreed? Good.

'Ross!' Julia Williams was back with her champion. 'I have something very delicate I want you to do for me . . .' and she explained the story of Becky's loss. 'I suspect Becky's lucky grass has been taken to put her off in her first big outside event with Kaimanawa Princess. All of the club riders respect you and so I want you to put the word out that it has to be returned immediately.

'It was a nasty, mean thing to do, but I have no interest in finding out who the guilty party is and nor should anyone else. Now, let's get back to work.'

To be able to compete for the Champion Pony purple ribbon, Becky knew Kaimanawa Princess had to be on the national register, which she'd done some time before, through the pony club, and she had already been given her competitor number for the day. She knew this was probably the only chance for her and Kaimanawa Princess to win the top junior riding honour — as Princess had never been entered in outside competition before, she would be eligible for the Maiden events.

She decided she would give them the best chance by paying her dollar entry fees for Best Groomed, Maiden Pony (ponies 14.2 hands and under), Maiden Pony Best Paced and Mannered while later in the day she would put herself forward for Best Rider over Fences for contestants aged between twelve and thirteen years, the Maiden Pony Hunter and finally they would tackle the Dual Jump event with Megan and Pixie.

But it was almost impossible to concentrate on the competition ahead when her mind was in such a confused blur, reliving every moment of their arrival to the time when she had tied up Princess to walk the course with Megan.

If she could only remember who was clustering around them . . . and more to the point, who in the pony club could possibly know about her lucky tussock grass and that she kept it inside the little pocket she'd sewn onto the blanket?

Megan could be a bit of a chatterbox, but when it was really, truly important she would never have betrayed this special secret. Becky was sure of that, and neither would Rachel, the only other friend she'd told about her grassy secret weapon.

Then she remembered with an uncomfortable feeling that Rachel had once begged for a few strands of the tussock grass to bring the same good luck to her and to Queenie when they were riding — at the time Becky had said she wasn't breaking up Bill's carefully tied little cluster of tussock grass for anyone or anything.

Roughly, she pulled herself together. Shame on her for even thinking such nasty thoughts about Rachel, one of her best friends. Get a grip, Becky told herself!

She had completed three preliminary rounds in the flat classes when Ross cantered up to her on Tara and muttered, 'Hold out your hand, Becks,' placing the small bundle of tussock grass in her palm. 'No questions, but here's your lucky grass and I've been promised that it won't ever happen again. If I were you, I'd use this as the best motivation to go out and ride the butts off every-one else and good luck to you both.'

Walk, trot, canter in the circle — who would believe this beautifully turned out model pony had been roaming wild only a year or so before, too feisty for Mr Jackson to even try and handle?

And now here she was at her first big event, the Western Bay of Plenty Gymkhana. Already she had been presented with red ribbons for Winner of Best Groomed and Maiden Pony in the show ring, and Becky was beginning to think they had a chance of winning her final event of the morning in the Maiden Best Paced and Mannered. If she did, the dream title of Champion Pony would be within their grasp. It was probably too much to hope for, but if the rest of their results were as good as the first three, Becky and Princess could be in for an exciting afternoon.

The break for lunch saw Becky fussing around her pony at the water trough before unsaddling her and tying her up in the same cool spot under the trees.

She glanced across at her clubmates. Despite what Ross had said, she couldn't stop wondering which one had stolen her lucky tussock. Who was avoiding her stare? No one. They all smiled brightly and congratulated her on her and Princess's performance as though nothing had happened. Well, maybe that was best.

Just forget it and concentrate on the first afternoon event — Best Rider over Fences — that would show everyone that it wasn't just Kaimanawa Princess who had real ability. Rebecca Mitchell, pony club rider, had what it took to be a winner too.

Meanwhile, in the lunchroom of the gymkhana grounds the three judges were holding an unexpected conversation. Their cups of tea had cooled and their club sandwiches were temporarily forgotten as they discussed the subject uppermost in their minds.

Was that charming little black pony with the white socks really a wild Kaimanawa horse? And could they honestly award the prestigious Champion Pony ribbon to a breed that had never before competed at this level?

'I've never even seen a Kaimanawa horse before today!' one judge laughed. 'Is she correctly registered to compete? Pass over the latest New Zealand Equestrian Federation registration book, Jan, and I'll do a quick check.

'Yes. Here she is: "Kaimanawa Princess". That's interesting, she's the only horse in the NZEF register with a Kaimanawa breed status.'

'You can't not give the champion's ribbon to her and her rider Rebecca Mitchell,' Jan Mountford objected. 'She's won fair and square in the events for Champion Pony, no one else comes near her and we can't let a narrow snobbish prejudice against wild horses prevent her from beating the thoroughbreds. Just think of how she performed in the Maiden Pony Best Paced and Mannered — those circles and the correctness of her canter — it was perfection!'

'I don't and can't agree.' The third judge was firm. 'What would that do for the whole pony club movement if some horse from the back of I-don't-know-where costing next to nothing is seen to head off more expensive thoroughbred ponies and horses? It would produce chaos. We could end up with half-breed draught horses competing.'

Both women laughed. 'Don't be silly! Let's just watch her performance this afternoon over the jumping events and keep an open mind.'

The lunch break was over. With a quick touch of her tussock grass for luck, Becky saddled up Princess for her own big test of the day — Best Rider over Fences for twelve and thirteen year olds.

She would be up against the top young riders of the province, like Erin Short, the Rotorua champion, and some tough contestants from her club including Danielle and Jackie but, to her relief, Megan had opted to compete instead in the next event, the Eyeopener.

Breathe in calmly, long breath out . . . right. An encouraging pat for Kaimanawa Princess, whose eagerness to compete had her almost jumping out of her skin, and then they were off for their round the ring jumping . . . *there must be no time faults, no baulking at fences, keep an even pace, don't take off for the jumps too far away, keep a good position in the saddle, think ahead and, above all, work together*. Becky repeated over and over to herself again the instructions Mrs Williams had given her so many times in preparing for this event.

Thank goodness she was going early — the tension of waiting to watch the others would have killed her.

Becky needn't have worried. Her little champion proved

to be just that, stretching her head and neck out as they approached each jump, while Becky had to admit she was riding to the top of her ability, with her body in a good forward position and her head up as she whispered words of encouragement in Princess's ear as they flew around the course.

It felt like a perfect round, so now she would just have to watch and wait . . . Danielle seemed to be off her stride, making the sort of errors she never had before while Erin looked good but nothing special. Perhaps, Becky grinned, she was just being extra picky.

'Best Rider over Fences — Rebecca Mitchell on Kaimanawa Princess,' the gymkhana's loudspeaker boomed out. A judge stepped forward to present Becky with her fourth red ribbon of the show, saying, 'Well done, Rebecca, you are certainly riding well today. I look forward to your next two events.'

How did she know that? There were so many contestants in the events, Becky could hardly believe that someone as important as a judge could be interested in her or her horse.

Amazing, but nice, and now after only one more event, they were entering the Maiden Pony Hunter followed by the Dual Jump.

Adrenaline and pride would have to get them there as horse and rider were both running out of energy.

They had to compete over four hurdles and here came the first hiccup of the day. Rushing into the third hurdle, Kaimanawa Princess clipped the rail slightly. It wobbled but remained intact. Then the fourth, cleared immaculately for a second placing in the event.

Now for the Dual Jump. Megan and Becky fidgeted as they waited for their turn. Would Pixie and Princess remember all their drills they had done together as they rode in unison over the three barrel jumps in the circle?

They knew it was going to be a hard contest, especially when they watched an earlier entrant ducking out of a jump and leaving his partner and rider stranded.

'Just concentrate, girls!' they urged their ponies as they nosed forward into the ring. Two black bodies with white flashes jumped in clockwork rhythm as their white-helmeted and navy-coated riders held their positions in precise formation.

'What a sight!' Toni Mitchell enthused as, flushed and happy, Becky and Megan dismounted. 'Your ponies looked spectacular and you both rode so well. If the judges don't award you first place for that effort I'd say they've got rocks in their heads! Only two more pairs to go and judging by their past records I don't think you've got anything to fear from them.'

'Hold the pose right there!' Not one, but two press photographers had lined up Becky and Kaimanawa Princess for a sequence of victory shots after the presentation of Champion Pony purple ribbon at the completion of the day's events.

'Plus, I want the photos to show all five of your winners' ribbons and the second placing as well as the champion's ribbon, lined up and tied around her neck,' one called out.

Rachel raced back to grab the ribbons that were hanging — in the pony club tradition — from the rear view mirror of the Mitchells' car, towing their float.

'Here you go,' she panted as she reached up to Becky, as the photographer took his shot. The Chief Judge was being interviewed by journalists from both the local paper and a horse magazine, whose writer was already gushing over the feats of Kaimanawa Princess.

It was to be her magazine's next lead story and Kaimanawa Princess would probably also feature on the cover. The journalist beamed. 'I can't believe this little pony once roamed the wilds!'

The judge nodded in agreement. 'Yes. It's quite staggering. We checked it out today during lunch and confirmed she is the first Kaimanawa horse — and only recently registered with the New Zealand Equestrian Federation — to receive the Champion Pony award at any event, anywhere in the country.

'If this is any guide to the future, I'm sure we'll see more Kaimanawa ponies achieving all sorts of goals at pony clubs throughout New Zealand.'

Patting her pony's back and sides, and so happy she could hardly think straight, Becky trotted Kaimanawa Princess back to the float where her parents were waiting to hug her. 'Wow!' Bruce Mitchell laughed. 'I'll think twice before I argue with you over a horse again, Becky — that was a day of sensational achievement!'

Becky jumped down and covered her horse's nose with kisses. 'We've got to get you unsaddled and back home now so you can tell your mum how clever you've been and Mr Binks — he'll want to know all about it.

'My darling little Kaimanawa Princess, you've just given me the proudest and happiest day of my whole life and you've earned us lots of money from your wins which I'll donate back to help save your relations and horsey friends in the Kaimanawas.

'And guess what? I've just heard that we've been selected for the Bay of Plenty team to compete in the National age-groups for showjumping. But this is a secret. The judge told me I wasn't to tell *anybody*, so you can't tell Queenie either!'

As the crowd and the floats streamed from the gymkhana grounds, Julia Williams walked over to Ross, who was brushing down Tara.

'Well done Ross, as usual, another couple of first placings to add to your tally. Look, I've told you I don't want to know who took that bit of tussock grass from Becky. But I am curious about how you got it back so quickly.'

'Simple, Mrs W.' Ross grinned. 'I just went over to our group and said I'd watched the grass being taken from Kaimanawa Princess's saddle blanket and if it wasn't given back to me pronto, I'd tell everyone at the pony club and at high school who'd done it. Becky's pretty popular and it was great the way she got her revenge in the best possible way.'

He'd watched the tussock grass being removed! Julia Williams smiled. 'That was so lucky.'

'Actually, I didn't see a thing,' Ross confessed with a wide grin, 'but the guilty person wasn't to know!'

Part Two

Chapter 7

Plants or horses?

*It's wild volcanic country, it's a prehistoric
terrain. But the terrain is fragile according
to conservationists and now the choice has
to be made as to which will survive — the
ancient plant life-forms nestling within the
vast 700 square kilometre land mass that
comprises the Kaimanawa mountain range
or the beautiful animal that has come to
live on it . . .*

— TVNZ documentary

But as Becky and Kaimanawa Princess were riding to
victory, the row between the two groups fighting over the
horses' future was becoming white-hot in its intensity.

At its centre stood a scientist whose work on the army's land at Waiouru in the southern area of the Kaimanawas had triggered the argument between the horses and the land, and whose study of the plateau land had first raised the concern about the horses.

The land forms and plant life of the Central Plateau survive from a prehistoric time when the territory rose up out of the sea and it was these precious plant habitats he wanted to protect, he told a gathering of angry horse-lovers. 'One is the basin tussock land, the other, the wetlands . . . there's only a handful of each left and only certain plants can grow there, some of which are very special.'

One called out from the back of the room, 'You don't know about the horses, you just know about the plants! All this protection for two little plants!'

The man was quick to defend his stand: 'One of these plants has only been seen in one other place in the country. The plant may have died out — there might be a total of ten plants comprising a one-metre radius in this whole area. It's an amazing plant that survives under water for six to eight months of the year.'

'Why not stick a fence around these plants if they're in such a small area?' objected a woman seated near the front of the room.

'I can't see any reason why the horses can't be kept in the wild and managed,' yelled a man.

Ignoring their shouted comments, he continued: 'The plant won't survive trampling. It needs the protection of grasses, dandelions and clover, which of course are what the horses graze on. We give this place a very special environmental value because we know of no other place in the North Island where this species occurs.'

It was the inaugural meeting of the Kaimanawa Wild Horse Preservation Society and the proposed round-up and auction of the horses had provoked the gathering, after animal welfare organisations made the issue a nationwide argument. 'I'm not convinced that culling or killing, as we call it, is the right thing. The proper place for horses is on the range,' objected a horse-lover.

Another spokesman followed the first speaker and said they were caught in the middle of the fight. He said that his job was to look after the land, but because they were protected by the law, to look after the horses too.

'The solution for us is to try and find some way to limit the impact of the horses on the special plants and the habitats that are important, but also to find some way of managing the horses, so that the values of the horses are retained as well.'

Then came an Army spokesman, who spoke of the need for the army to have unimpeded access to nature's rifle range in the Central Plateau. 'This has got to be one of the best training areas in the world. It's very big and it offers a great range of terrains. It's well suited to our business.'

Horse-lovers trusted neither the army nor the conservationists, claimed a large man sitting in the centre of the room. 'We suspect a conspiracy between you lot! The army wants the horses gone and the debate about damage to the land is just a camouflage.'

Not true, the army man retorted. 'They are an inconvenience and that's a product of the size of the hoof, but no one wants to shoot horses and we go to great lengths to avoid doing that, so one of the problems we have is clearing the horses from the range area.

'The horses themselves are pretty smart and have an incredible ability to hide themselves in the low ground — they could give our soldiers lessons!'

Bowing to environmental pressure, the National Government lifted the protection status of the horses through a Parliamentary Bill passed in May 1996 and announced that the first kill of approximately 1000 horses — two-thirds of the total wild horse population — was to go ahead just four months later, in August.

The Kaimanawa Wild Horse Preservation Society never knew that it had so many friends. And, as word spread about the threatened killing of the wild horses, more New Zealanders were joining its ranks each day and offering to sign one of the society's petitions to prevent the slaughter.

Becky and her family began to follow the story that

was unfolding through the pages of the newspaper and on television. One afternoon, Toni handed her daughter a copy of the local paper when she arrived home from school. 'Have a look at this love, while I make you something to eat. It's more about the Kaimanawa horses.'

Becky sat down at the kitchen table and started to read an interview with the chairman of the Kaimanawa Wild Horse Preservation Society. He'd taken a handful of Kaimanawa horses to show the crowds attending Waikato's Mystery Creek Field Days and then on to the centre of Hamilton, to continue their horses' campaign.

'This is the first time the horses have been seen in public,' he said. 'We were a bit worried about whether they would behave themselves in the city, but they were great. People were amazed at how beautiful and tame they were and you can imagine they attracted a lot of interest — and signatures for our petition!'

Asked about the claim from the Department of Conservation that the horses needed to be killed to protect several species of tussock grass, he said he disputed that theory. 'I believe one type of tussock grass in question is dying from fungus, not from any damage inflicted by the horses. I've asked the Department of Conservation to test the grass for fungus but we get no reply to our requests.'

He also said a census of the horses must be taken. 'The numbers just aren't there for a kill, or a cull as they call it. No one knows how many horses there are — we can't get a straight answer when we ask about why they object to doing a census.'

Becky read on, as her mother quietly put a mug of hot cocoa beside her on the table. The chairman ridiculed the idea that in a cold winter less tussock would lead to the horses' starvation and that the killing would be humane and in the horses' best interests. 'That is too silly to comment on — the horses have got along fine there for the past 120 years. Why should this winter be any different?'

He had flown over the area in a helicopter. 'A huge area was agreed on for the horses to have but later we found it had been reduced by half. Likewise, we later went in and looked at the land which was used by the horses and well nourished, but four days later another interested party was taken in and shown another place with barren land and told that this poor tussock growth was because of the horses!'

Later that night the family watched as a TVNZ documentary added its weight to the argument:

'. . . ecology is not simple. Horses have been part of the human story for many thousands of years. We used to depend on them but now they depend on us for survival — perhaps that's why they inspire such strong feelings.

'These wild horses and foals are roaming free in the Kaimanawas. They've never seen a stockyard fence, never been touched by humans . . . it's the very centre of the island — 700 square kilometres. This is a landscape with a violent history and nearby are

112

its makers — the volcanoes of the Central Plateau that created and recreated the contours of the land over thousands of years. The horses arrived with the Europeans in the nineteenth century, now they have been 130 generations in the wild before they have had to compete with men . . .

'A man from Forest & Bird says, "Wonderful as they are as we see them streaming across the tussock land they are in the wrong place." The horse lobby disagree. For them the welfare of the horses is the issue. "Our view is that the horses belong out on the range," they say.'

Rachel was on the phone. 'Becky, can I ask you one big, big favour? My nana grew up with horses and she's been reading all about the hassle with the Kaimanawas. I go on about Queenie all the time till everyone's sick of listening, but Nana can never hear enough about you and your farm, Princess and Queenie and the pony club. She says she's never seen a Kaimanawa horse and would love to stroke one before she dies! She's going to sign the petition to help save them, too.

'You know how Dad got the council's permission to have Nana's little Lockwood house moved over from Thames into our back yard, well it's here now and looks really nice. She's happy because her old cat Cindy has moved over from Thames to live with her and she's got her own home and we've got ours — but she still does our washing and cooks all our meals and spends most evenings with us.

'Anyway Nana's invited you and Queenie to ride over for a home-made afternoon tea this Saturday at her house. Would it be OK for you to come?'

Yes, that would be fine, Becky said, she'd look forward to it. Clip-clopping along the country roads on a horse was really relaxing as long as she stuck to the grass verges and there were no stupid hoons tearing around in their old bombs for Queenie to shy at. The two of them would be there around three, she promised. 'See ya!'

It was a bit funny, she thought as she saddled up Queenie to ride her over to Rachel's house on the fringes of town. Princess looked put out too. Becky grinned as she stroked her pony's nose. 'Look, sweetheart, your mum's the star today. You've had enough fame for a while and if you get bored here you can always make eyes at Binky in the paddock!'

It was a sunny winter's afternoon as she and Queenie cantered into town and, for at least the hundredth time, Becky thought how lucky she was to have bought Queenie — it was the best $50 she'd ever spent. She had turned out to be quite a star like her daughter but in a different way.

Kaimanawa Princess was the champion but Queenie's nature was so sweet and nice that she had now got her own little fan club with the children who came to ride her weekly at the pony club, and of course with Rachel, who was completely besotted.

Becky jumped off Queenie as she opened the gate to Rachel's house. Her friend ran out to meet her and wrap her arms around Queenie, before planting a big kiss on the mare's nose.

'My two best friends have come for tea!' Rachel's face was all happiness. 'Tie Queenie up to the fence post here and come inside to meet Nana. She can't drive any more because of her eyes, so it's a real treat bringing Queenie to her instead.'

Rachel's grandmother was short and plump, with friendly shiny dark eyes like a couple of blackcurrants, Becky thought. She smoothed her hands along her apron and grasped Becky's hand in both of hers saying: 'I know how kind you have been to my granddaughter in sharing your lovely horse with her and by making it possible for Rachel to learn to ride. Riding was my life as a kid growing up at Tokomaru Bay on the East Coast, because it was our only way of getting to and from school every day. We used to ride bareback, my big brother up the front, my little brother in the middle and me at the back and when we got to school, we'd tether him up to the hitching rail under the trees behind the classrooms.

'Our horse was called Prince and when he wasn't taking us to school or being ridden to the general store to do some errand for Mum, Dad had him working as his farm horse. I loved our Prince — and now I'm going to meet a Queen!

'Give me your hand, dear, to help me walk down the steps — one of the disadvantages of getting old is that you get a bit wobbly on your pins — so that I can see this beautiful mare for myself. I've never ever seen a Kaimanawa horse but of course we knew all about them when I was growing up.'

It is said that dogs and cats always know when they meet a person who loves them and so it is with horses.

Queenie, who had been eyeing a nearby plant as her next meal, switched her attention to the old lady who was now caressing her and uttering soft, loving words in her ear. 'You're a beautiful girl and what a lovely face and markings you have,' she murmured to the horse. 'This afternoon our special tea is for you, too, Queenie, not just for Becky and Rachel.

'I've cooked a special treat for you and there will be enough left over for Becky to take home so that Kaimanawa Princess and Mr Binks can have a share. I don't want anyone feeling left out today!'

They sat around the kitchen table as Laura Montgomery reminisced about her country childhood so many years before. How, when she was eight years old and sick with tonsillitis she'd had to ride seven miles — 'I don't know how far that is in kilometres' — over hills and country tracks to get to the doctor. 'I was feeling really crook and then I had to ride all the way back home again on my own on dear old Prince, clutching my medicine in a dark bottle. I do remember it tasted evil, but I suppose it helped me get better. I'll never forget that painful journey . . .'

On the table Rachel's nana had laid out freshly made fruit scones with great chunks of plum jam and whipped cream, some pikelets Rachel had helped her make, with home-made strawberry jam, and lemonade to wash it down.

It was all delicious and all too soon it had to come to an end. 'I'd better get Queenie home before it gets dark,' Becky said, as she rose to her feet. 'You don't know who's zipping around on the roads and I don't want her to get frightened.'

Mrs Montgomery gave Becky a hug and handed her a large brown paper bag of horse treats. 'I'm going to stand at the front door and watch you and Queenie as you trot down the road. How I miss riding horses and what wouldn't I do to stop these lovely little fellows, like Queenie, from being destroyed by the officials.

'Sometimes I think the world's gone mad. If there's anything I can do to help save the Kaimanawa horses just let me know — I'll sign petitions and do anything I can to help. Thank you again dear, for coming over and making my day.'

Mrs Montgomery had put the thought in her head. Was there something practical *she* could do to help save the horses, Becky wondered as she rode back home. She'd put it to the family that night as they had their evening meal. You never know, someone might come up with a bright idea.

'Umm,' was Tim's offering, Steph ignored the question and said what she wanted was more pudding, and her parents stared at her blankly. 'What can ordinary people like us do? What could a thirteen-year-old do?' they asked.

'If the government's made up its mind, no matter what the people want, they'll just shove it through.' Bruce reached for another slice of bread. 'Tell you what, though, I read in the paper a couple of days ago that the guy who organised the muster when we got Princess and Queenie is going to be in charge of this next one. This time he says he's upgrading the stockyards he built for last year's round-up and as well as mustering the southern region, he's predicting a big round-up in the north.

'He says he wants to work the horse bands together into a mob, to terrify the horses with the noise of the helicopters roaring overhead so they'll gallop down the final bank and into his stockyards.

'The new stockyards are being built in a blind gully and the only way forward is into the pen. The plan is that the leading stallion will lead the mob towards a gap he sees in the fence and while they're whinnying and rearing at the front, the fence will have been closed on them . . .'

Becky didn't want anything more to eat — she felt sick. Perhaps it was the big afternoon tea, perhaps it was what her father had just told her. She pushed her chair back and ran from the table to seek the refuge of her bedroom.

She climbed into bed to snuggle under her duvet and then as she had done months earlier, Becky reached into the top drawer of her dressing table to clutch at Bill's tussock grass.

She closed her eyes. *Please. Let something be done to save our horses of the tussock country and let there be something I can do to help . . . I will do my best, that I promise.*

There was one New Zealander who wasn't prepared to wait around and see what could be done. Bob Kerridge, executive director of the Auckland Society for the Prevention of Cruelty to Animals (SPCA) gave vent to his views in the SPCA's magazine *Animals' Voice*.

'On a broad scale few animal issues have disgusted me as much as the Kaimanawa horse scam. In this issue we are dealing with an undeniable hidden agenda which, despite protestations to the contrary, is to eventually be rid of the herd . . . against this scenario is the overwhelming evidence presented by international and local experts that killing is unnecessary and inhumane, supported by public concern of such dimensions as we have not experienced before.

'We have the feeble reasons as to why . . . a danger to traffic (you would be lucky to see one, let alone hit one in your car) . . . the need to protect our special tussock (all 70,000 hectares of it?) . . . and more latterly the threat that for the first time in 120 years they'll starve to death in winter (a statement would you believe attributed to the SPCA)!'

He continued. 'The international listing of the protection order covering this unique breed has been arbitrarily lifted without consultation to allow an open killing season and the Department of Conservation has approved the elimination of some 1000 horses without even an accurate idea of how many horses remain . . .'

Bob Kerridge urged his readers and the people of New Zealand to contact their local Members of Parliament, the Army and Parliament itself to put an end to the potential extermination. 'The arrogance of officials must not defeat the compassion of caring individuals to save these unique, proud and beautiful Kaimanawa horses . . . we will, of course, continue in our efforts, with your help.'

His words were followed by an action box, with a small form to be sent to the Minister of Conservation stating *'We urge you to stop the unnecessary killing of the wild horses of the Kaimanawas, and return their protected status by legislation'* to be signed by readers and then sent to Parliament House in Wellington.

Her coffee had brewed and its heady aroma had permeated throughout the kitchen and into the hall of her wooden villa. It was Sunday morning and the favourite day of the week for Julia Williams. No work, no pony club duties, no housework — just a pleasant, lazy winter's day ahead with as much time as she wanted to browse through the Sunday papers and then take a long ride along the sands on Barney, her hunter.

The rain that was beating against her windows made a cosy morning inside even more attractive and, better still, she knew the weather forecast had predicted it would clear up later in time for her ride.

A headline in the *Sunday Star-Times* caught her eye. 'They shoot horses don't they?' Anything to do with horses was sure to grab her attention and this headline was no different.

Pouring out a large mug of coffee and planting herself down in a deep comfortable armchair, Julia began to read. The opinion column had been written by a well-known journalist, Frank Haden, and it started with another question: 'What in the name of all that's unholy has got into the Department of Conservation with its mad scheme to shoot the wild horses of the near-desert country of the central North Island?

'For most of us the horse is special, even more revered than the dog and the cat —' Yes, she could certainly go along with that, Julia nodded as she read on. 'Humans simply love horses. They envy their grace of movement. They regard the friendship of a horse as a privilege. No decent person would shoot a horse unless it is badly hurt or suffering . . . yet they (DOC) not only plan to go ahead with the slaughter, they keep trying to pretend in the face of the mounting evidence it is necessary.

'It isn't. The rubbishy land the horses have been living on for more than a century is too poor for farming, the fact that the horses have accommodated themselves to the harsh environment is a tribute to their toughness. They have earned the right to live out their days in peace . . .

'DOC must not go ahead with its mad plan. In plain English, it doesn't know what it is doing. There are far too many unanswered questions, too many acknowledged experts who disagree violently . . . other countries exploit their wild horse herds by making them a tourist attraction.

'Our bureaucrats, if we let them get away with ignorantly exercising their power, will brand New Zealand in the eyes of the rest of the world as the place where "They shoot horses don't they?"'

Well. That was her day of peace and relaxation gone. With her heart pounding in agitation, Julia re-read the article. It made even worse reading the second time around and as she poured herself another coffee, Julia's head raced with the thoughts that were tumbling around her head . . . of bay, chestnut, and black horses with their manes tossing as they roamed the wild tussock land, of Queenie's patience with the special needs children who so loved her — like the silent little girl whose face lit up with joy whenever she was placed on the back of the mare — of Kaimanawa Princess's great intelligence in mastering the skills of competitive riding disciplines and horsemanship within a matter of months, skills that took other horses years to achieve . . . it made her really mad just thinking about it.

But what difference could she, one woman, make? Well, she could do something and if everyone who cared did something — who knows where it would lead? Julia reached for a notepad and her pen and began scribbling little headings down under the words *Actions to take to save the horses.*

She had seen a small advertisement in a recent horse magazine inviting people to donate to the cause or to get petition forms from the treasurer of the Kaimanawa Wild Horse Preservation Society who was based in Rangitikei. She would hunt out the magazine and the name of the contact person and ask her to send as many petition forms as they could spare.

Then she would spend the rest of the morning on the phone calling up all her horse contacts, asking them to accept petition forms and to then get them filled out and returned to Parliament as soon as possible.

But first she would telephone Becky, as it was thanks to her that Julia was about to become involved with the campaign. 'Hello, Julia Williams speaking. Is Becky there? It's rather urgent.'

What could have happened now? Becky dashed to the phone after her mother had called her to come quickly to speak with Mrs Williams.

There was nothing the matter, Julia said after hearing Becky's anxious voice, 'Apart from the fate of the Kaimanawa horses that is and I know how concerned you are about that. I've decided I can't sit back any longer doing nothing so I'm about to organise as big a protest as

I can from this district. I'm about to get a pile of petition forms sent up here and then we need to get them signed and returned to Parliament.

'The more people we can get to sign, the more powerful our voice will be. Aside from my own friends, I'm going to ask our pony club members to take the petitions around . . . Ross to the seniors at high school, Megan to the convent, you for the juniors at the high school and so on. I'll ask our people from the special needs groups to add their weight to the cause for saving the horses — and that's all thanks to your Queenie.

'But there is one more thing that I really need to get those petition numbers up,' Julia said after a pause, 'and I don't know who to ask.

'I want to set up a stall in town for people to sign the petition. To do that we need to find someone, perhaps an elderly person, who has the time to spare and the commitment to sit there all day and get people to sign. But who? Everyone who I know either goes to work or school or is too busy on their farm to spare the time . . .'

'I know just the person.' Becky felt happier than she had for days. 'She's already told me she wants to do something to help the Kaimanawas and I know she would be just perfect because she loves horses. It's Rachel's nana!'

'I'll call Rachel right now,' Julia promised. 'And when it finally stops raining go out and give those two Kaimanawas of yours a big pat and a piece of carrot each from me.'

Chapter 8

The battle rages

*And so the battle rages. Horses, landscape
and the army — how to make room for all
three in the Kaimanawas?*
— TVNZ documentary

Late at work one night in his Auckland office, Roger
Ginsberg, the senior art director of a large advertising
agency, was flicking through the back issues of the *New
Zealand Herald* looking for an article he needed for a
new campaign. But instead he found he kept stumbling
on news stories about the Kaimanawa horses.

Why they captured his interest was something of a
mystery as he knew nothing about them, apart from
driving along the Desert Road and seeing the road signs

advising people to look out for the wild horses in case they ventured onto the road.

But Roger was an animal lover and the more he read about the horses and the fate in store for them, the more annoyed he became. The original article he'd been hunting for was forgotten. It was time to go home and talk things over with his wife Sue and see what they could do to help the horses.

Home for Roger and Sue Ginsberg was a vibrant menagerie of humans, animals and birds all happily living together under one roof — three daughters, several rescued and SPCA cats, Deakon the dog, a much-loved kune kune pig, a pet bird who chattered away in their living room and Roger's 'son' and only male companion in the household — a large turtle who spent his days sitting on rocks or ambling around under the leaves and plants of their garden.

As they sat together at the dining room table that night Roger told Sue about what he had read. 'I'm really upset about this plan to kill those beautiful horses. It's wrong. I think that being in the sort of business I'm in, I should — and can — do something about it . . .' and with that a whole new commitment and chain of events began for the Ginsberg family.

Like Julia Williams, the Ginsbergs decided to draw up their own plan of attack to help save the horses.

Words and design work were Roger's weapons, while Sue decided she would get organised and take a *Save the Kaimanawa Horses* petition around the streets of their suburb as well as set up a stand at the monthly Saturday market. 'There are always lots of people at the market and I know we'll attract plenty of support there for the horses.'

It was time-consuming collecting signatures, as each one involved a long explanation and a conversation with the person she approached, but it was rewarding to watch those sheets filling up — she had no doubts about that.

Many people didn't know the horses were about to be killed and were very shocked when they found out, she told Roger after one long rainy day spent at the village market with Deakon patiently sitting at her feet as she endlessly repeated the story of the horses.

'They'd hear me out, sign up and then say to their friends, "Hey come and sign this", and we would get more signatures! I struck one nasty person who was rude and said it was a good job the horses were being killed, but he was an exception. Most people were great.'

Her daughters had been 100 per cent behind their parents in their support for the petition and that day's work in the rain, added to all her other days, had taken the number of signatures she had collected to more than 400 — not a bad effort for one family, she thought.

Now it was time to send the forms off to Wellington. 'I hope the politicians really listen, and don't just accept them politely and then ignore the whole thing,' she said to Roger, in a gloomy moment.

'Whether they admit it or not, the politicians will

be taking notice,' Roger assured her. 'Don't forget the general election is less than three months away — and that's what counts for them. They would be foolish to go against a popular cause that could put them at risk of losing the election.'

In the Bay of Plenty the petition sheets were filling rapidly, Laura Montgomery saw with satisfaction, and there was an unexpected benefit as she sat there patiently with her papers, hour after hour, in the local shopping centre. She was meeting lots of people and making some new friends.

Two ladies who signed up for the horses had invited her for afternoon tea when she finished her work with her petition sheets and another couple had asked her to join them at the local indoor bowls club, saying, 'We live close to you. We'll pick you up and drive you there and back home afterwards . . .'

Somehow leaving Thames didn't feel like such a big sacrifice. She loved her grandchildren and her son but she was lonely at times, missing her old friends. Now here she was living in her own home again, with dear old Cindy to sleep cosily on her lap and making some nice new friends. That made her feel very happy.

Across town, Julia Williams was also experiencing an unexpected pleasure as she handled all the petition forms she'd sent around the local horse-loving community. Above all, she realised, she was helping many people who felt frustrated that they couldn't do anything practical for the horses.

'I've felt so helpless about all of this,' one friend explained. 'I can't imagine our local MP taking the slightest notice of anything I've got to say on a national issue. Now, by signing your petition, Julia, I feel as if I'm actually doing something to help the horses, which our politicians won't be able to ignore.'

The pony club members had done wonders too, Julia noted, as she scanned the petition lists that were finding their way into her letter box almost on a daily basis.

The high school alone had produced almost 500 signatures, which amounted to more than half of all the pupils and staff in the school, and added to Mrs Montgomery's contribution which carried about the same number of signatures, things were heading for a magnificent contribution from their small town.

A month later the Ginsbergs had another brainstorm session about what further action they could take for the horses. Words were the way to go, Roger said, but it would probably cost them thousands of dollars.

The best thing to do would be to place a strong,

emotional full-page advertisement in the newspaper which they would have to pay for themselves. 'If you're up for that kind of action and financial commitment, Sue, I'll draft up something and then we'll decide how and where to go from there.'

Sue agreed, but when they admired the impact of the finished product when it appeared in the front section of the paper, Roger said, 'This is all well and good, but it only appears once. I get the feeling that it's like a fire building — and I think that we need to do more.'

Then, from nowhere it seemed, Roger had another idea. Why on earth hadn't he thought of it before? He worked in advertising after all — so why not take the campaign one stage further and make a television commercial that could reach into every New Zealand home, urging people to stop the killing of the horses?

The difficulty was that a commercial would be horrendously expensive. Saving horses couldn't be claimed as a charity and the TV stations weren't going to run it for nothing. Paying for the commercial would cost far more than the Ginsbergs could afford. 'I'll sort this out later,' Roger decided. 'That's another problem! I'll make the ad first, then something will happen and we'll be able to do it.'

He was working on another advertising project with a photographer who wanted to direct his own TV commercials so he decided to start with him.

Roger sounded out his friend and got an enthusiastic response. 'Oh, yeah for sure, I'd love to direct it,' Dave replied, adding he was certain that Ziggy, his new business partner and a fine cameraman, might also like to be involved.

Yes, came back the prompt reply. Ziggy was keen to work on the project.

OK. Roger went back to the newspapers and looked up the names of the horse groups who were at the heart of the struggle, to see if he could find some contacts and then make a phone call or two.

By now the argument was becoming news and the number of wild horse support groups had grown. There was the International League for the Protection of Horses, under its patron Dr Ian Shearer, a former government cabinet minister; the Kaimanawa Wild Horse Action Network; WHOA — the Maori Wild Horses of Aotearoa organisation, who wanted to develop eco-tourism with wild horse watching from 4WDs on their land; the Wild Horse Trust; and, from Switzerland, the Franz Weber Foundation, who were offering to buy all the land that was needed and all the wild horses to keep them protected for ever.

Where to start? Roger photocopied dozens of newspaper articles and spoke to a number of the people involved without having any clear idea of what direction his commercial should take.

Then he read one news clip which captured his imagination. That was the perfect way to tell the story — a Kaimanawa horse, a young girl . . .

How could Roger contact Becky and her family and ask to shoot the TV commercial with her horse, Kaimanawa Princess? All he knew was that they lived somewhere in the Bay of Plenty and that Kaimanawa Princess was a prize-winning pony, he explained to the secretary of one of the horse groups.

'Those two would be perfect for our campaign,' Roger enthused. 'If you can get back to me as soon as possible with her family's details that would be good. Tomorrow would be fine, but tonight would be even better!'

The following morning Toni Mitchell was astonished to receive a phone call from a stranger who introduced himself by saying he was in advertising and he would like to come down from Auckland to their farm, with his film director and a cameraman, to make a commercial to help save the Kaimanawa horses, using Kaimanawa Princess and Becky.

Well, yes, she would have no objection to that and she was sure that when Becky arrived home from school she would give it her 100 per cent support, Toni said, adding that her family were as upset as everyone else in the horse world about the proposed cull. 'We think it's cruel and unfair.'

Good. But as it wasn't a paying project, they would have to come down in their own free time, Roger added. 'And as time is running out we'd like to come down this weekend. Which would suit you better, Saturday or Sunday?'

The answer to her prayers — Bill's chunk of Kaimanawa tussock grass had worked its magic once again! After making a phone call to Roger to confirm that Sunday would suit them, Becky punched the air for joy, rejoicing that some kind-hearted advertising men from the city were giving her the opportunity to fight in the best possible way for the lives of the wild horses.

She was just a kid and didn't understand the rights and wrongs of saving plants or the ecology of New Zealand, but she did understand that she wanted to do whatever she could to save a thousand beautiful horses like Princess and Queenie from a horrible death.

Armed with a rough script for the commercial, the advertising trio set off with their ideas and camera equipment for the Bay of Plenty in the small hours of Sunday morning.

They knew it was going to be a long day, as all three men were perfectionists and determined to do the best they could for a highly unusual project that had no financial backing and no guarantee of ever running on television.

'How in the heck are we going to make this happen, Roger?' Dave asked as they nosed their way through a foggy patch on State Highway 27 on their way to the farm.

'I'm not sure yet,' Roger admitted, 'but it'll be good, everything will turn out just fine. Trust me.'

Meanwhile, at the Mitchells' farm it was almost impossible for Becky to stop herself from bubbling over with excitement. In her riding gear, she roamed restlessly between the house and the horse paddock as she waited for the men to arrive. Fortunately, the early morning fog had lifted and a bright winter sun shone down in its place.

Kaimanawa Princess had been groomed for the biggest day of her life and the jumps had been placed strategically around the paddock for prime action shots. But sensing Becky's restlessness, the three horses were whinnying and pacing around and that wouldn't do at all. Becky decided she'd better move Queenie and Mr Binks to the paddock that was half hidden behind the trees, where they wouldn't be a distraction to Kaimanawa Princess or the film crew for the job ahead.

And the excitement she was feeling didn't just belong to Becky, her family and the horses. Julia Williams had asked if she could come to the farm to supervise the riding sequences, Megan had promised she would be over on Pixie to watch the day's filming and Rachel also said she would ride over on her bike during the morning to catch the action.

The men arrived shortly before nine, took a quick look around the paddock and the rest of the farm including the river, then settled in for a hearty breakfast, while they discussed their plans for the day with the family.

'The finished commercial will only be about one-and-a-half minutes, or two minutes long at most,' Roger warned, 'but the filming could take all day and long into the evening to get everything we'll need. We'll end up editing out about 95 per cent of everything we shoot, but it's so important that we get it right that it'll take all of that time. Is that OK with you guys?'

The Mitchells agreed — it would be a long exhausting day but Becky knew instinctively her pony would rise to the occasion. She had never let Becky down before and she wouldn't let her down today.

'She's a really awesome little horse and she'll do whatever you want,' Becky promised. 'We've painted up some placards that say *Save the Kaimanawa Horses*! I'll carry a couple of them out to the paddock if you want to use them for the ad.'

Good idea. Dave suggested that they might introduce the commercial with Becky holding one of the placards. 'That would let people know straight away what the ad is for, taking them right into the heart of the issue.'

One more time over the jumps. It felt like they had repeated this sequence about fifteen or twenty times,

Becky thought wearily, but this time it was Mrs Williams who was demanding that the sequence be re-shot, saying, 'You didn't look quite crisp enough, Becky, as you went over that jump — I noticed that Princess hesitated slightly in the approach.'

Megan and Rachel, who were leaning on the fence behind the cameraman, both grinned. They were secretly relieved they weren't being asked to go over and over the sequence of shots that would make up the commercial.

Becky looked over at them and grinned back, knowing what was going through their minds. But, hey, her friends didn't have the privilege of being able to shape events for the horses either, she reminded herself.

She was the truly lucky one, and as for Kaimanawa Princess, well she was just awesome — never once baulking at a jump, or dawdling in the trot — doing exactly what she was asked all day long.

The pony had stood as steady as a rock when Becky was asked to hold her bridle in one hand and one of the placards in the other, as she looked directly at the camera and described the emotional moment when she had first seen and chosen Kaimanawa Princess among the horses of that first muster.

'Let's go down to the river,' Roger suggested. 'I think we can get some excellent shots and I'd like to get some of her running free and wild — no saddle or bridle or any of that stuff, just free — through the bush alongside the river bank.'

Another group of sequences and it was time for a

tea break. Leaving Kaimanawa Princess watered, fed and tied up to her post, everyone trooped back to the house for ham sandwiches. But they'd been beaten to the punch.

'Naughty Fluffybum!' Toni yelled crossly as she led the way to the table. 'Steph, I told you to keep your cat out of this room — just look — all the ham's been picked over and chewed by those little teeth! Bruce, start slicing some more ham,' she said. 'Roger, I'm so sorry, this is going to delay the filming.'

'No worries,' he replied. 'We'll be refreshed by having an extra few minutes here. Sometimes it helps the creative juices if you sit back and have a rest in the middle of all that concentration.'

'Does it take this long to shoot all commercials?' asked Megan, whose cousin was a photographic model. She was starting to have second thoughts about her dreams of following her cousin into the same glamorous career. 'How on earth can your models stand around all day in those really high heels while you go over and over the same scenes?'

'Well, don't be deceived by those long slender bodies,' Roger laughed. 'Models have to be pretty strong, you know! We shoot most commercials in sections so it isn't always as tough as today's work has to be. Come to think of it—' he paused, '—we might even hop down to the Central Plateau to get some shots of the mountains where the horses live . . . hmmm, we'll have to think about that guys.

'But for now,' Roger rose to his feet, 'I think it's time we got cracking again, folks, and finished off the commercial. Thanks for the nice fresh ham, Bruce!'

'No thanks to Fluffybum,' Tim grinned. 'I don't think Mum would appreciate that. She spent ages arranging the ham so carefully just to impress you guys!'

It was almost dark as the three men walked back to the paddock. 'What a great light for mood shots,' Ziggy said, looking around him. 'Perhaps we don't need to travel south to Waiouru. We can probably capture the right sort of mood here.'

Her friends had long gone as Becky mounted Kaimanawa Princess for the final shots of the day. Her pony should have been exhausted by the stop-start sequence but somehow she wasn't, performing like a true champion.

They raced through the final takes and now it was time to allow Queenie and Mr Binks to join their friend. 'Wow, we should have included her ma too!' Ziggy said when Becky told him about her. 'She's not a bad looker.'

'Don't even think about it.' Roger shook his head. 'We've got tons of good footage to work on and it's long past our time to be heading back home.

'So long and many thanks,' he called to the family, as the men slowly steered their way from the paddock and out onto the farm road. 'We'll be in touch in the next few days to tell you how the ad is looking and when it's going to show on TV.'

Good question, the men quietly reflected to each other

on their journey back to Auckland. When — and more to the point *where* — was their commercial going to show free of charge on nationwide TV?

As Roger had said to himself when he first dreamed up the concept, he would worry about that problem later . . . the only thing was that with so little time left to act, it had to be sooner rather than later.

Chapter 9

TV star

'Many of the world's wild horse populations are only partly wild. Most are managed herds like the Camargue in the south of France, where the numbers are controlled, and their behaviour is affected by this. Not so the Kaimanawa horses.'
— *TVNZ documentary*

Their ad was emotionally right and hit the spot, the team agreed, as Dave showed Roger and Ziggy the finished product two days later. It captured brilliantly the feelings of a young girl, her much-loved pony and national uproar in the helpless sense of anger being experienced by many at the destruction of the wild horses.

Now, the next challenge they faced would be to enlist the support of someone influential in television circles who would be prepared to stick his or her neck out and run the two-minute commercial free of charge during New Zealand's prime-time nationwide 6 p.m. news.

Roger made an appointment with a television manager he knew and asked if he would run the advertisement. 'Look,' he said, 'we're onto the hottest issue in the country! I'm offering you a unique film clip of a kid with the first-ever gymkhana- and national showjumping-winning Kaimanawa wild pony. Your viewers won't be able to resist it!'

No, sorry. Someone had to pay for a commercial of that length and — as Roger had predicted — the manager closed off their conversation by saying, 'Sorry, mate, we're not running a charity.'

OK, OK. Would they let him speak to a friend in the TV studio who read the night's news, he asked? There would be no problem with that, the manager replied, and within minutes Roger was in his friend's office, clutching the video.

The two men sat in silence as the sequence rolled through. 'Oh, wow!' His friend was obviously moved by what he saw. 'That's really powerful stuff. Perfect. Yeah! Look, leave it with me. I'll think about it and come back to you.'

The following day Roger was back in his friend's office. His friend came straight to the point. The news wasn't great, but there was something they were prepared to do to help the cause.

'Look, we want to run it but we can't — it's just too long!' the newsreader told him. 'It's two minutes something or other, but we can run bits of it for you guys.'

'No, no.' Roger was determined. 'It's just not going to work in bits, you know that. It's got to be run in total.'

'Ohhh . . . arrgh . . .' Roger recognised the signs . . . his good friend was weakening. 'Well, all right. You might get me shot like those poor damned horses, but we'll do it and I'll make sure it's run on the six o'clock news.

'To make sure it has the absolute maximum impact, we'll run it this Thursday — two nights before the first of the two big horse protests which are taking place on the Desert Road at Waiouru this Saturday and Sunday.'

'It would be really awesome if Becky and her parents could take Kaimanawa Princess in their horse float down to join the planned protests that coming weekend and it would be particularly good on Sunday because that would catch the attention of the national press for Monday's edition.' Roger was on the phone to the Mitchells to tell them he'd managed to secure a television slot for the advertisement.

'You'll be on television for more than two minutes on Thursday, on the prime-time news — just imagine that!' Roger told Becky. 'It's exactly what we wanted. Then it'll be followed up by the impact of Saturday and Sunday's protest, which I know will be covered in the press and on the radio as well as on TV, the following day. With a bit of luck that should just about nail it and stop these dreadful killings.

'I realise,' Roger added persuasively, 'that this will be another long day for you, your mum and your dad — not to mention Kaimanawa Princess — but we've come so far, we shouldn't stop now.

'And I happen to know from one of my friends who works at Parliament that the pressure is really beginning to hit home with the politicians. It could all be over by this time next week, so we need to move now.'

Four trained shooters had been put on standby to shoot the horses as soon as the weather was right during that month, it was reported in the press and — urged on by inflamed calls from talkback hosts throughout the country — phone calls, letters, petitions and faxes of protest bombarded Parliament on a scale never experienced before.

And the row was raging as fiercely within the government's ranks. On his regular Sunday talkback show on *Radio Pacific*, National's Minister of Tourism John Banks called for a minute's silence 'to reflect on the orgy of destruction that is soon to take place on the Central Plateau', adding 'I'm saying to people out there that there must be a better way than sending in gun freaks with high-powered machines to wipe out these horses.'

'This is coming as a roar from the heart right throughout New Zealand.' Roger was on a late-night call to his TV news friend. 'I can feel the anger out there just boiling over.'

They would be leaving home at 5 a.m. the following Sunday to get to the protest on time, Becky told Megan. 'Hey, Megs, would it be OK if you and I go for a ride on the beach on Saturday, the afternoon before we drive down?

'I'm so nervous about everything that's coming up this week and there's lots I want to talk to you about. It would make me feel heaps better if we can have a really good goss and then a race along the beach with Pixie and Princess.'

It would tire the pony out too, so that she wouldn't be so edgy travelling alone all that way in the float, Becky added as Megan said she'd look forward to riding with her friend.

'Megs, do you know what really worries me the most? Kaimanawa Princess really freaks out with any sudden noises or car horns.'

Megan could hear the worry in her friend's voice.

'And the guys who are organising the protest are asking motorists to honk their support for us as they drive past. What say my Princess gets terrified, bolts out onto the main road and is run over? I could never forgive myself if that happened.'

Murray Haitana was a farmer, whose Tuwharetoa people had lived in the Kaimanawas for many centuries. Out mustering in the ranges one day he was riveted by the sight of a wild stallion, who seemed to appear out of thin air, galloping straight towards him.

Amazed, Murray froze to the spot, as the stallion stopped suddenly, reared, rolled its eyes and neighed. Later he told a reporter from the *Kapiti Observer* newspaper that although he knew horses well, this was his first experience with the wild Kaimanawa breed — known as the wind eaters. He also told the reporter that the word Kaimanawa could also mean to eat one's heart.

'I was frightened but captivated by the sheer presence of his challenge. There was nothing I could do but stay cool,' he said. 'I rolled a smoke and watched. Having checked me out, the horse tossed his mane, snorted and turned, all in one fluid movement and was gone like the wind.'

It left him with a powerful image of freedom, and of how the horse was at one with that very harsh environment. Ever since that day he had carried a torch for the protection of the Kaimanawa horses. 'I can understand DOC claims that their increasing numbers endanger the fragile eco-system of the high country, but after more than one hundred years of survival they belong to the land. That's what I saw in that stallion,' Murray Haitana said. 'They are tangata whenua.'

He said that he and a partner wanted to develop an eco-tourism venture, which would include rides along the old stock trails Maori used to evade the colonial army and settlers — providing windows into some of the North Island's most magnificent landscapes.

'The history we would tell would include the amazing but sad contribution of the Kaimanawa horses to the war effort,' he said. 'About 8000 horses accompanied New Zealand soldiers to the Boer War, another 10,000 in the first landing at Gallipoli alone. In those days the army didn't supply them — New Zealand's volunteers had to take their own horses and most were sourced from the wild. And of those many thousands of horses, only four were brought back to New Zealand. How tragic is that?

'We continue to ignore the amazing contribution of the Kaimanawa. No one has researched the contribution of this animal to the building of this nation, its early economy and its impact on our culture.

'The only monument to the Kaimanawa horses who took part in the war was a statue in the North Island town of Bulls. It showed Bess, one of the four horses to come back from the war. The army had agreed for a later Anzac Day service to allow members of the Queen Alexandra Mounted Rifles, supported by several air force officers, to honour the memory of Kaimanawa Bess with a twenty-one-gun salute,' he said.

'It is time that we as a nation, both Pakeha and Maori, eat our hearts and recognise the Kaimanawa as a national taonga, a treasure.'

Murray Haitana's views were echoed in the press by Moa Larkins, who had featured in a number of celebrated horse rides, one alongside Sir Howard Morrison throughout the length of New Zealand.

He said he'd worked closely with Maori groups and had been interested in the welfare of the Kaimanawa horses for years. 'I count a day as incomplete without at least a couple of rides on my horses. I believe there must be thought given to the long-term management of the herd in the wild because I see the protection of the horses' well-being as absolutely paramount. I want to be allowed to do a ground observation of the horses as soon as the New Zealand Army will issue me with a permit.'

Meanwhile The International League for the Protection of Horses was demanding that a census be carried out by experts everyone could trust before the shootings started, and its patron, Dr Ian Shearer, was lobbying hard behind the scenes with his former government colleagues to halt the killings.

From Switzerland, the animal welfare organisation, the Franz Weber Foundation, was firing off faxes and letters to New Zealand authorities and Bob Kerridge of the SPCA, saying they had the funds to pay for the land and the horses to keep them safe as a herd for the future, and only needed the go-ahead from the government for the cheque to be sent.

By way of explanation, Franz Weber confirmed to the government that the foundation was for the conservation of wildlife, nature and environment with its headquarters in Montreux, Switzerland. It had a membership of 230,000 and was experienced in creating and running wildlife sanctuaries.

She was the last person on earth Becky expected to see approach her on that Thursday lunchtime at school. Danielle was heading in her direction — no mistake about it.

Then came the next shock. 'Hey, um, Becky, can I talk privately with you for a minute?' Danielle looked nervous. Becky had never seen Danielle nervous about anything.

Curious, Becky shrugged. 'Yeah, OK. What is it?'

'Um.' Danielle's head went down. 'There are a couple of things I want to say. I heard you're going to be on TV tonight with Kaimanawa Princess so that's awesome. It really makes me mad that they're planning to kill those Kaimanawa horses and I think what you've achieved with Princess is so good.

'I didn't at first, but you know that. I was a real pain about her because I thought you couldn't get a good horse so cheaply. I also wanted to say good luck for the protest on Sunday. Jackie's told me that you and your mum and dad are driving down to the Desert Road for the day.'

'Thanks, Danielle.' Becky turned to leave.

A red-faced Danielle grabbed her by the arm. 'There's

something else I've got to tell you and I'm so ashamed. Promise you won't tell anyone?

'It was me who took that tussock grass from the saddle blanket at the gymkhana. I'd seen you touching that bit on the blanket every time you rode Princess in a competition at the club and I knew that whatever was inside must be important to you, like a lucky charm . . .'

Becky felt a rising anger surging through her body. She'd always suspected Danielle of stealing her lucky grass and now here was the proof. Unable to speak, Becky looked at the ground as Danielle, in tears, continued. 'I knew Kaimanawa Princess would become better than Rajah because of her jumping. Becky, do you have any idea what it's like to be an only child with parents who want you to achieve all the time?

'They give me everything I want but I'm expected to win everything too. I get silly, nasty little comments when I miss out.' Tears were pouring down Danielle's cheeks. 'Do you honestly know what it feels like to live with that? But they're my parents and I love them and I want to please them.

'They're so proud of me and what they paid for Rajah to help me win competitions. They keep telling me that one day I'll make the Olympics but I know I never will because I don't have your guts at the jumps. There, I've told you.' Danielle brushed her hand across her eyes and abruptly turned back towards the classroom block. 'I'm really sorry and good luck for this weekend.'

'That's OK, Danielle.' Becky's anger had disappeared

as rapidly as it had come. 'Thanks for what you've just told me. It'll stay our secret.' The two girls managed a smile. They could never be friends, but they could now live with each other.

Rachel had been an enthralled onlooker, watching from a distance while the pair were talking and as Danielle walked off, she rushed up to Becky. 'What on earth was that all about?'

'Um,' Becky hesitated. 'She was just wishing me good luck for Sunday. Danielle's not so bad really, just a bit stuck-up.'

Rachel glanced sideways at her friend. Tears, heads down and that kind of body language didn't look like any kind of good luck wish to her, but she couldn't worry about that. She had more important news.

'Hey, guess what, Becks? Mum rang last night and asked Dad to come up and see her this weekend to talk things over. She says that living in Auckland isn't what everyone cracks it up to be and she's missing us all. She told Dad she's decided she wants to come back home.'

'Wow!' What a stellar lunch hour this was turning out to be. Becky grabbed her friend's arm. 'That's the best news! How does your dad feel?'

Rachel shrugged. 'He's OK with it. But he told Mum that whatever happens between them now or in the future, Nana is staying — no argument — and Mum said that was fine by her. She said she likes going out to work better than doing the cooking or housework, so she reckons it could work out pretty well for everyone in the family with Nana at home and her out at work.

'There's only one thing though, Becky.' Now it was Rachel's turn to look nervous. 'Do you remember when I cut my birthday cake at your house and Tim said I was allowed to have two wishes? Well, now they've both come true and I wanted to know if it would be greedy to still ride Queenie and belong to the pony club?'

'Of course you're not being greedy, silly!' However could Rachel think that her mother coming home could change anything between them? 'You're going great guns at the pony club and Queenie . . . well, Queenie's your mate for life.'

Her heart was beating so fast she thought it would pop right out of her chest. Becky looked at her watch for the umpteenth time and saw the six o'clock news was only six minutes away. 'Hurry up and come into the lounge everyone,' she yelled. 'We're just about on!'

Like more than a million New Zealanders, the Mitchells sat glued to the screen as TV's lead newscaster announced the news for that evening Thursday, 1 August 1996. Fidgeting, they paid little attention to the night's lead story of a major riot overseas before the news broke off into the first ad break.

'Here we go!' Unbelievably, what they had lived through less than a week ago was unfolding in front of their eyes — the Mitchells' farm and the river,

Kaimanawa Princess breaking through the trees to run free along the river bank, Becky and her Princess working at the jumps, Becky and the pony walking — and all as a backdrop to a sombre voiceover on the screen:

In the next few days the bloody slaughter of the Kaimanawa horses will begin.

DOC and the Minister of Conservation, Simon Upton, have decided that up to 1000 horses will be herded down and shot or, as the Minister calls it, removed.

The International League for the Protection of Horses wants a moratorium on the kill, so that all the factors can be considered and alternatives examined. For example a contraceptive programme for the wild horse population is being trialled by Massey University, and some of the horses could be rounded up as in the muster in 1993.

One of those 1993 horses is Kaimanawa Princess and now she's owned by a thirteen-year-old girl and not only part of a team who are the national showjumping champions in their twelve to thirteen age group, but also ranked as third in the world.

Ask yourself, is the slaughter the only way to go? Only luck has saved Kaimanawa Princess from the hunter's bullet. Hundreds like her will not be so fortunate.

Please write or fax the Prime Minister's office and tell him that if one single shot is fired National will not get your personal or party vote in this election. Perhaps the thought of being removed from office will cause Mr Upton to reconsider his decision.

The Mitchells' phone was going crazy. Toni Mitchell handled some of the calls then Bruce took over, Steph got to speak to school friends who phoned to say they'd seen them on television and Becky felt as if she'd spent the whole night on the phone.

Julia Williams had called to congratulate her, Rachel and her grandmother were next, Megan was in for a long session and even Ross Edwards, who Becky had always been slightly in awe of, wanted to chat.

'Good one, Becky,' he spoke in admiring tones. 'You handled that really well. A real pro. And I'm sure your lucky grass wasn't too far away when you were shooting the ad. Tell you what, I'll buy you a milkshake to celebrate your stardom next time I see you in town.'

But the Mitchells' friends weren't the only ones to react instantly to the powerful, emotive commercial.

At Parliament's Beehive building the Prime Minister and several close colleagues were in urgent talks that had started at the end of the news.

'Hi there, superstar!' As Becky galloped up to Megan, her friend volunteered, 'Dad reckoned seeing you on TV on Thursday will turn the tide. He says he thinks you're onto a winner taking Kaimanawa Princess down to Waiouru tomorrow because everyone will want to photograph you. You're famous. Gimme your autograph!'

'Don't be silly, Megs,' Becky laughed. 'The horses haven't been saved yet and they say the kill is only days away. Let's hope the protest works out OK.

'I've never been so nervous in my life, but then I've never been as committed to anything before either. Anyway that's tomorrow and today's today. Race you to the end of the beach!'

They'd had the best workout in the nearest thing to a race tie they had ever galloped and now they were back in their favourite place, sitting under the pohutukawa trees with the horses' bridles tied up to the low-lying branches.

'Well, what's the goss you promised to tell me?' Megan stretched forward lazily.

'There wasn't anything much then when I rang,' Becky confessed, 'but there is now. Rachel came up to me at school on Thursday and told me that her mum's coming home to live with them again.'

'Tell all!' Megan commanded.

Half an hour later they scrambled to their feet and brushed the sand off their seats, ready for the ride home.

'Hey, do you remember this time last year when we found those kittens here?' Becky asked. 'Well, Fluffybum's a real character. The other day he ate the ham for the TV guys' lunch which made Mum mad, and he really loves Binky. He likes to run along the top rail in the horse paddock, right up to where Binky's standing and then he pushes his head against Binky's nose for a rub and a love.

'He'll sit there for hours just watching or trying to play with the horses. So how's things going with your two?'

Spoilt as, Megan admitted. 'Midge and Maggie sprawl out in the middle of Mum and Dad's bed every night. Dad grizzles like crazy about that, he says he's a farmer in charge of a couple of hundred cows and yet his life is ruled by two pint-sized cats!'

The girls had reached the junction in the road where they rode off in separate directions back to their farms. Megan leaned forward in her saddle and waved an arm. 'Good luck for tomorrow, mate, I'll be thinking of you. And have you got your lucky tussock grass sitting safely in your saddle blanket? Because I've got a feeling you and the Kaimanawa horses are going to need it.'

Chapter 10

Showdown on the Desert Road

Where was she? It was pitch black, the air was icy cold and someone was shaking her shoulder.

'Becky, wake up! It's time to get dressed.' There standing by her bed was her super-supportive mum, already up and dressed at 4.30 a.m. and, Becky knew, with a hot breakfast waiting for her on the kitchen table.

Mmmm. Another five more minutes more, Becky begged sleepily. 'Just one more little wriggle under the blankets while I wake up properly. Gosh it's cold—'

'Yes, it is dear. As well as your raincoat, I want you to stick on your thick black jersey over your skivvy because it's going to be freezing cold down there standing around on the Desert Road. And don't dilly-dally around in bed because we've still got to get down to the paddock and load Princess onto the float.'

Must remember to put Bill's tussock grass in her pocket, Becky reminded herself. Get up now, get dressed and then put that precious little lucky talisman inside one of the pockets of her jeans. Put on two pairs of thick woolly socks to keep her feet warm through the long hours of standing on the road verges and, finally, on with the most comfortable trainers she owned.

Queenie was the first to neigh with surprise as the headlights of the Mitchells' car shone through the blackness at the paddock.

'Becky, hop out and stick the halter on Kaimanawa Princess and then lead her into the float,' her father asked. 'It's far too dark out here to put her protective boots on. We'll drive until the dawn breaks and then we'll stop to do it. My only hope is that she behaves herself alone in the float for that length of time.'

Becky stroked Princess's head and muttered reassuring words as she slipped over the halter, but as they walked towards the float the teenager laughed to see they had company.

'Hey, Queenie and Binky, it's still bedtime for you two! Sorry but this is one journey you can't come on.' Becky gave the two older horses a pat.

'But I promise you, Queenie, we're going down there to try and save lots of your friends. We'll do our very best for them and I hope we can come home with good news.'

As the chill winter's dawn transformed itself into daylight, the Mitchells gazed at the road ahead as they talked nervously about what lay in front of them that day.

Toni had packed them two large thermos bottles of tea and coffee in a carrier bag, with sandwiches and scones to keep their spirits up, and she suggested as they drove through Taupo that it was time for them to have a short break.

'Princess is being pretty good compared with how she usually travels,' Bruce commented as the car and float pulled up at the roadside on a rough patch of grass. 'I think we'd better check on her too.'

'Do you somehow understand you're on a very important mission?' Becky teased as her pony stood in her travelling stall more docilely than the Mitchells could ever remember.

'Or do you just have an instinct in that beautiful black head of yours that you're close to home in the Kaimanawa mountains and you're feeling pretty happy about that? Whatever's affecting your mood, baby, keep it up because we're nearly there.'

Shortly after nine that morning they pulled up on the outskirts of Waiouru to join the group of protesters organised by the Kaimanawa Wild Horse Action Network, who were already massed at the roadside. They were armed with banners reading 'Don't Kill the Horses' or

'Protect the Kaimanawa Horses' and were in no mood for compromise.

'We'll do everything we can to prevent them from starting the kill,' one girl confided as she introduced herself to Becky. 'Good on you for bringing Kaimanawa Princess down to the protest. After that neat publicity you got for the horses on TV the other night you're just what we need to be the front person for this campaign.'

Honk, honk. A car flashed by with four occupants giving the protesters the thumbs up. Honk, honk, honk! This time a long-distance truck. Honk, honk. And another.

Becky glanced nervously at Kaimanawa Princess. What on earth was going on? There she was standing as calm as could be, with her head held high in a scenario that would normally freak her out and have her bolting for cover.

'I just don't understand the attitude of why they would kill these beautiful horses for some tiny plant.' A protester shook his head as he chatted to Toni and Bruce Mitchell. 'Surely the army have done as much, or more, damage than the horses. If they're out there doing manoeuvres, isn't that harming the grasslands?'

Other protesters added their comments too: 'That botanist guys says the blame is with the horses, but we don't believe him. Who says the horses are doing the damage that this botanist claims?'

'Have they ever put up traps in that red tussock area where the flora is and checked that there aren't a million rabbits going in and out?'

'Why don't they have enclosures for rabbits and horses and find out what damage each causes? Don't want to, I suppose.'

'And what about the pine forests that were planted out to the west of the army land, but the wind has blown the seeds east! It's costing tens of millions of dollars to clear the pine plantations from the land and they're still there! What kind of damage have those trees caused to the land? No one's talking about that!'

The talk was going on and on and everyone was getting worked up.

Becky walked away from the growing group of protesters to face the road alone with her pony. Honk, honk! It was the best reaction she could ever imagine. Everyone travelling on State Highway 1 that day seemed to be on the horses' side! Honk, honk!

And her brave Kaimanawa Princess standing there so proudly alongside Becky, hating what she was living through, but never once flinching from the roar of the vehicles or the strident sound of car horns piercing the air.

Becky felt a rush of tears spring up in her eyes at what her pony was having to endure. 'I love you, Kaimanawa Princess,' she whispered softly into her horse's ear. 'Look up now to the hills beyond the road — that's where you came from and your family, all those stallions, mares and foals up there, that we're trying to save. But I think you sort of know that, don't you?'

Kaimanawa Princess gently nuzzled her head into Becky's shoulder. And then — tossing her mane — she gave out a whinnied cry of anguish that penetrated right across the Waiouru valley and from there deep into the heart of the Kaimanawa mountains.

The horses nibble on the trees and shelter under them in the snow that lies deep on the ground in the Kaimanawa Ranges.

From the Argo Valley in the South to the Maori lands of the North, the heart of winter in the Kaimanawas is a time to endure, a time to eat the wind. The foaling season is still months away, and the close-knit bands of horses stick close together.

Those near to the army camp hear the warning call from one of their kind. They go on alert. The stallion rounds up his family and prepares to move them to higher and safer ground.

'Hello, girlie, thought I might see you.' Becky swung around at the sound of a familiar voice. 'Bill! How fantastic — you told me we'd meet again but I never thought it would be here. Guess what's happened to Princess since you left us . . . '

Bill tipped his hat on one side and grinned lazily as his

161

young friend regaled him with her pony's great deeds. 'Said she would be good, didn't I? Now have you still got that tussock grass I gave you?'

Becky fished in her jeans and pulled out the grass. 'I never go anywhere without it — it's my lucky grass. I've even had a little pocket stitched onto my saddle blanket, Bill, so it goes with me to competitions at the pony club and the big ones, too.'

Queenie was having a good life she said, helping kids with problems at the pony club and she'd become her friend Rachel's horse. 'Mr Binks likes her too. In fact, everyone likes Queenie.'

'And she only cost fifty bucks,' Bill mused half to himself. 'I only hope some of her mates are as lucky.

'We've talked long enough, girlie.' Abrupt as ever, his mood had changed. 'It's too damned cold to be standing still and, like you, I've come a long way to be here today. Let's make sure those so-and-sos don't win this battle. Give me one of those protest banners of yours and I'll start shouting for the horses, too.'

Kaimanawa Princess had faced people shouting alongside her, cars and trucks honking their support and now there were camera flashes going off in her eyes. The press and television cameras had arrived and it seemed everyone wanted to profile the pony and her young owner from the Bay of Plenty.

'Kaimanawa Princess is the first horse of its breed to win titles at a New Zealand provincial gymkhana and then in the national showjumping team event for twelve- to thirteen-year-old riders. Is that correct?'

'Yes.' Becky beamed as she described a dream sequence after winning the Western Bay of Plenty Champion Pony event. 'We were selected with two other riders from the Bay of Plenty for the nationals and Kaimanawa Princess just stole the show. She didn't put a hoof wrong all day! I love her and I'm so proud of her.'

Was the horse growing nervous at all the noises going on around her today, another asked?

'No it's amazing, quite spooky, in fact,' Becky told the news reporter. 'I know this sounds funny, but it's almost as if she knows what's going on. She is an awesome horse, so intelligent. She has the most common sense and I know she trusts me about what's going on today.

'There's another thing, too. Usually she kicks up a real racket about riding in the horse float, especially when she's travelling on her own and we always have to bandage her legs so she doesn't do herself an injury, but today for some reason we can't figure out, she's just been an angel. As I said, it's quite spooky.'

Final question. Did she think the protests would be enough to save the Kaimanawa horses?

Instinctively Becky touched her jeans pocket. 'I hope so. Everyone seems to be on our side, which makes me feel good about it. My friend's dad reckons that the politicians wouldn't dare go ahead with the killings with an election so close.'

'Good logic,' the journalist agreed, and laughed. 'Well, you've got plenty of friends who are on your side, that's for sure.'

'You'll be featuring in the national press and on TV tomorrow,' said another journalist. 'And I've just learned from our Parliamentary reporter that 500 letters were delivered to Parliament yesterday, and that's not counting the thousands of faxes that are cluttering up the works at the Post Office. So you've got the numbers. Good luck to you both.'

It was dark and their day's work was over. Bruce, Toni and Becky were on their way home with Kaimanawa Princess safely in the float. The day had gone as well or even better than they had hoped for and they were all exhausted.

They had done what they could and now it was over to bigger and more powerful forces than the Mitchells to decide on the horses' fate.

The message came through to Becky in her classroom just before lunchtime the next day. Would Rebecca Mitchell please report to the Principal's office as soon as the bell rang for lunch.

What had she done wrong? Had something happened to the family? Forget the lesson she was supposed to be taking part in — the request put her mind in a spin. The Principal had never spoken to her since she had first started at high school earlier that year — what was so important that he was asking her to go to his office immediately?

With her heart beating fast Becky walked down the corridor and knocked on his door.

'Come in!' a voice boomed out.

Nervously she opened the door to see a tall man standing in front of his desk. Then to her surprise he reached out his hand towards her. 'Let me be the first to shake your hand and congratulate you, Rebecca Mitchell of Form Three!'

'What's happened?' Becky asked in bewilderment.

'I've just heard the midday news on the National programme and the lead announcement is that the Prime Minister, Mr Bolger, has announced that the cull of the Kaimanawa horses has been called off at the eleventh hour!

'Well done, Rebecca, for your fine efforts to save the horses. You are a great credit to our high school and I will make an announcement to this effect at our school assembly tomorrow morning.'

'*Wow*!' Becky couldn't restrain herself. 'That's the most awesome news, sir! Thank you so much for telling me.' And walking from his office with as much dignity as she could manage, Becky raced down the corridor to find Rachel and tell her.

Unbelievably, they had done it! Between them the New Zealand horse-lovers and their friends had pulled off what had felt like the impossible and saved the horses! All those petitions, meetings, faxes, letters, publicity and most of all her darling horse had worked and forced the government to change its decision. It was just awesome!

Caught in the traffic of Auckland city, Roger Ginsberg punched the air with delight as his car radio brought the news that the horses had been spared.

'Yay!' Roger yelled ecstatically to the astonishment of the occupants of the car waiting alongside him for the lights to change. 'We did it!' I must get on the phone to Sue, Dave and Ziggy to share the news with them, he thought.

The horse-lover groups were delighted at this 'triumph for common sense' they said in a series of press releases that were hastily fired out to the media — in favour of a muster and horse auction the following autumn.

This was, they said, an opportunity to begin the in-depth study of the horses they had been seeking all along. They also demanded that protection status that had been lifted from the animals earlier in the year be restored.

A television documentary was to be made on Becky and Kaimanawa Princess and a team would be coming down to film them at the farm later that week, she was told. As wonderful as all that was, nothing could match Becky's excitement and pride that her pony, once so shy and nervous, had helped to save her wild friends in the Kaimanawa Ranges.

She walked down to the paddock with three large chunks of carrot. One for Mr Binks, one for Queenie. And a specially large one for Kaimanawa Princess.

She talked to her as she was saddling up for a ride at the beach.

'Today it's just you and me, Princess,' she said as she stroked her pony's black mane. 'I know we've got lots of adventures ahead of us, but I don't think that anything will ever be as good as this one.

'Your brave stand on the roadside at Waiouru is really going to be something to tell your grandchildren!'

The rain lashed against their faces as they galloped along the deserted beach, the horse's mane flying in the wind as the raging surf pounded against the shore.

This may not have been the freedom that Kaimanawa Princess had been born to, but it was a freedom and a friendship just as precious . . . the enduring bond of a girl and her pony, completely at one with the other.

Paddy the Wanderer
Dianne Haworth

He was everybody's friend on the Wellington waterfront, the big brown dog with the friendly grin and floppy ears, and they named him Paddy the Wanderer.

When a heartsick young Airedale began roaming the streets looking for his little mistress in 1928, he began an amazing journey that would take him around New Zealand, across the Tasman and into the heart of a city.

On the run from the dog-catcher, Paddy was adopted by taxi drivers and watersiders who bailed him out. He ran alongside them in the Wellington riots and when he went missing, they searched for him far and wide.

This is the true story of an amazing dog with a taste for adventure, who brought joy and laughter during the dark days of the Depression and became a much-loved sea-faring legend.

■ HarperCollins*Publishers*

The true story of a dog who
captured the heart of a city

PADDY
the wanderer

EXTENDED
EDITION

DIANNE
HAWORTH

Paddy the Wanderer
Extended Version
Dianne Haworth

This extended edition of *Paddy the Wanderer* includes maps, photographs and new stories about Paddy, which came to light after his story was first published in 2007, when it became an instant bestseller.

Dianne Haworth is an author, dog-lover and editor of *Animals' Voice*. She lives and works in Auckland.

HarperCollins*Publishers*

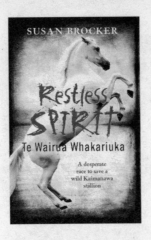

Restless Spirit
Susan Brocker

A restless spirit roams the slopes of the snow-topped volcanoes and the harsh tussock landscape — a wild, white Kaimanawa stallion who cannot be tamed.

Lara is new to the town beneath the mountains and hates it; Kahu is one of her new classmates — outwardly cocky and confident but troubled by his own self-doubts.

Hunters slaughtered the young stallion's family, teaching him to fear and distrust humans. But when a brutish trainer targets him during the annual muster, he must trust Lara and Kahu if they are to have any chance of saving him.

Before they can help the white stallion, Lara must overcome her anger and Kahu must find the courage to reveal his hidden talent. Hardest of all, they must both face the reality that to help the stallion, they may ultimately have to lose him.

■ HarperCollins*Publishers*

Pony Club Secrets 1
Mystic and the Midnight Ride
Stacy Gregg

Issie loves horses and is a member of the Chevalier Point Pony Club, where she looks after her pony, Mystic, trains for gymkhanas, and hangs out with her best friends.

When Issie is asked to train Blaze, an abandoned pony, her riding skills are put to the test. Can she tame the spirited new horse? And is Blaze really out of danger?

This is the first in the exciting new Pony Club Secrets series by Stacy Gregg. With gymkhanas to win, rivals to defeat, mysteries to solve and ponies in danger to save, these books are perfect for all girls who love ponies.

HarperCollins*Publishers*

Pony Club Secrets 2
Blaze and the Dark Rider
Stacy Gregg

Issie and her friends have been picked to represent the Chevalier Point Pony Club at the Interclub Gold Shield, the biggest competition of the year, and it's time to get training.

But when equipment is sabotaged and one of the riders is injured, Issie and her friends are determined to find out who is to blame. With a little help from Issie's old pony, Mystic, maybe they can solve the mystery.

■ HarperCollins*Publishers*

Pony Club Secrets 3
Destiny and the Wild Horses
Stacy Gregg

Issie and Blaze were hot favourites to win the Chevalier
Point Pony Club dressage competition, but now they have
to spend the summer on Issie's aunt's farm instead.

During her stay, Issie overhears a conversation about
plans to cull a group of wild ponies, and she is determined
to find a way to save them. Luckily she can call on her
pony club friends, because Issie is going to need all the
help she can get.

HarperCollins*Publishers*

Pony Club Secrets 4
Stardust and the Daredevil Ponies
Stacy Gregg

Issie has landed her dream job, handling horses on a real film set, and with a group of frisky palominos to deal with, Issie asks her friends at pony club to help out too.

But it's not just the horses who play up on set — what is spoilt actress Angelique's problem? Could this be Issie's chance for stardom?

Join talented young rider Issie on another action-packed adventure from the Chevalier Point Pony Club.

HarperCollins*Publishers*